METEOR

THE SKY IS FALLING

J.D. MARTENS

EPIC Escape

An Imprint of EPIC Press
abdopublishing.com

The Sky is Falling
The Meteor: Book #1

Written by J.D. Martens

Copyright © 2018 by Abdo Consulting Group, Inc.

Published by EPIC Press™
PO Box 398166
Minneapolis, MN 55439

Cover design by Candice Keimig
Images for cover art obtained from iStock
Edited by Amy Waeschle

LIBRARY OF CONGRESS CATALOGING-IN-PUBLICATION DATA
Names: Martens, J.D., author.
Title: The sky is falling/ by J.D. Martens
Description: Minneapolis, MN : EPIC Press, 2018 | Series: The Meteor; #1
Summary: Dr. Suri Lahdka and Dr. Robert Miller discover an icy body capable of destroying
    all life on Earth, but the United States Government won't let them publish their data.
    Meanwhile, when Jeremy Genser, High School Senior, discovers the truth, he and his
    friends struggle to come to terms with the world's possible demise in their own way.
Identifiers: LCCN 2017946135 | ISBN 9781680768275 (lib. bdg.)
    | ISBN 9781680768558 (ebook)
Subjects: LCSH: Adventure stories—Fiction. | End of the world—Fiction.
    | Meteor showers—Fiction. | Teenagers—Fiction | Young adult fiction.
Classification: DDC [FIC]—dc23
LC record available at http://lccn.loc.gov/2017946135

For Jake

*His wonderful ideas and insights into
astronomy made sure none of my
characters broke the laws of physics.*

1

THE WHITE DOT ON THE BLACK SCREEN

February 19, 2016
Soldier's Bar, Downtown Houston

"You'd think we would have noticed it sooner."

Dr. Robert Miller sat at the end of the bar, staring down his glass. Right now he was not the Director of the Astrophysics Department within the government hamster wheel that was NASA. He wasn't just another actuarial grunt for the government. No. Now he was Robert Miller at the end of the bar, just ordering another drink.

"I'll get this one," Dr. Suri Lahdka said, motioning her slim hand to the bartender.

"It's not like it really matters anymore anyway," Robert grumbled.

"Shh!" Suri said, "No one's supposed to know!"

Nearby, a man wearing a cowboy hat pricked his ears up.

Robert laughed at Suri's comment. "You think anyone will believe us? To them we're just typical liberal hippie crackpots."

The drinks came. To Robert they looked like a hangover, but to Suri they looked delicious. In reality, they looked like surprisingly strong appletinis.

Robert cupped the effeminate glass in his wiry hands, and in two big gulps the bright green liquid was gone.

"Okay." He looked at his glass bashfully before turning around to the dingy bar, raising his hands and his voice. "Okay! Everyone! I have an announcement."

"Oh no," Suri mumbled.

"The world is going to end!" Robert shouted.

No one so much as raised an eyebrow at Robert's yell. The bar, called Soldier's, used to be a joint Robert frequented often back before he stopped drinking. There he could drink in peace, since his coworkers would never go to the dreary saloon-style joint.

Robert tried again, standing on his barstool. "Citizens of Houston, we are all going to perish, but much before our time. The world is going to end, and it'll end in less than a decade!"

"Dr. Miller, maybe we should . . . " Suri said anxiously, noticing the bouncer making his move toward them.

"Nonsense! And Suri, you really can call me Robert. Or Rob, or Robby. What the hell do I care? The world's going to end." Robert grinned and raised his eyebrows comically.

Suri cringed.

"Alright, buddy, I think it's time to go," the disgruntled bouncer mumbled.

"Where can we go? A comet three times the size of the one that killed the dinosaurs is going to collide somewhere on the Earth, turning us all into stardust."

The bouncer rolled his eyes.

The man with the cowboy hat drinking Budweiser at the bar interrupted the conflict. He spoke up in a pure, calculated voice, and it had a dreadful finality to it: "By the sweat of your brow you will eat your food until you return to the ground, since from it you were taken. For dust you are and to dust you will return."

Genesis, Robert's foggy mind thought. He remembered his father saying those very words to him as a boy, when he was much too young to understand their meaning. Cowboy Hat didn't flinch a muscle when Robert snorted and laughed boisterously.

"Ah, yes, Bible freaks beware. It'll get you too. It's not just us heathens. We'll all be torched—"

And with that, Robert climbed off his stool and the bouncer escorted him outside. Suri hurried to keep up, knowing that Dr. Miller had just hit the nail on the head.

• • •

Eight hours earlier . . .

Dr. Robert Miller woke up in his Houston home in Midtown. He wiped the sleep from his eyes, and headed to the bathroom. He was fifty-six years old, had blue eyes sunk into their sockets, and was lean, but not skinny. His near-perfectly white hair had been that white for some twenty years; he had gotten used to it long ago. Back in the days of his PhD candidacy, he had resented it, and thought it meant that he was aging too fast. "It must be all the neutrinos," he used to joke to the lay people in his life.

Perhaps unsurprisingly, Robert kept few non-physicists in his life. He kept to himself and his work as the Director of Astrophysics at NASA. Like many at NASA, the "what do you do" question is great for bars and picking up girls, but the reality of work is much less exciting than the barroom fantasies.

Robert's current project was called Kuiper Search 15439. Robert led the effort to find life or anything interesting orbiting around the Sun in the area called the Kuiper Belt, a region past Neptune's orbit known for containing a lot of comets. In reality, however, he spent countless hours reading and coding line after line, looking at anomalies in statistics on the makeup of planets' atmospheres. Since modern modeling software was so advanced it could identify most data anomalies, Robert's job was to cross-correlate different data sets to determine if these anomalies were interesting enough to study further.

Robert sat in his car in the usual mind-numbing Houston traffic. He was only around five miles from Johnson Space Center, but it took around thirty-five minutes to get to his parking spot. Despite making top salary as the Director of the Astrophysics Department at JSC, he drove a modest 2015 Hyundai Elantra. He liked the car's interior, and the air conditioning cooled the car immediately—a lifesaver in the Houston heat.

After showing a few security guards his badge, Robert walked into his office and plopped down, emitting an audible *hmph* when his butt hit the leather chair.

His oak desk had papers strewn all over it. As a student, Robert always imagined he'd end up in a nice office with a crystal decanter filled with scotch. When he got his promotion to the "corner office" five years ago, his dream came true, and a nice assortment of crystal scotch glasses and a decanter sat inside a globe to his right . . . but since he had quit drinking it was purely ornamental.

To Robert's left was a tall bookcase filled with astronomy, astrophysics, astrobiology, and many other *astro-* and *-ology* books. A thin coat of dust had settled on all of them. The vast majority of his work was done on his computer—coding, looking over codes, answering email, and attending way too many meetings. Aside from all this, Robert coded and accepted or denied permissions to move various satellites and telescopes fractions of a millimeter to look at different areas of the sky. When he had a question that one of the books could not answer, he looked it up on one of the thousands of online databases he had access to.

Robert pulled up his email on his computer and sighed. Forty-seven emails in just one day! What a disaster; he wouldn't be able to do any meaningful work for at least another two hours.

Upon closer inspection, however, around fifteen of the emails were from a Suri Lahdka, whom he vaguely recalled hiring for her computer science potential. He remembered she was a bit frantic and neurotic, and this blast of emails confirmed that.

Suddenly, there was a frenzied knocking on the door. It wasn't a *knock-knock*; someone was rapidly punching his office door.

"Yes, yes! Come in, please."

To his surprise, it was Dr. Lahdka who entered, and she was very out of breath.

"Dr. Miller . . . Um. My name is Suri, sir. Suri La—"

"I know who you are, Dr. Lahdka. I hired you, remember?"

Suri blushed. "Ah yes, well. I've been emailing you, and I tried to call your cell phone but no one answered and you weren't replying to your email and I tried to find you on Facebook but . . . " Suri slowed to catch her breath, allowing Robert to speak.

"Suri, I'm going to stop you right there. You need to slow down. What is going on?"

"I'm not exactly sure. Did you check your email yet?"

Robert raised his eyebrows.

"Right, sorry. Well, I think I found an undiscovered comet."

Robert became annoyed. There were perhaps millions of masses in the solar system that were undiscovered.

"So, what? You want to name it after your boyfriend?"

"I don't have a—" Suri hesitated before continuing. "No, I don't. I think its trajectory could be . . . problematic."

Dr. Miller narrowed his eyes. "Problematic for whom?"

"I've been researching masses in between Uranus and Neptune, and I ran the N-body simulation to look at its trajectory over the next ten years."

With that, Suri opened her backpack and pulled her laptop out of its case. She logged in, and then into the JSC supercomputer. Robert put on his reading glasses, wearily inspecting Suri's findings.

"Right," he began. "Around forty kilometers in diameter, unnamed. Origin: Kuiper Belt. Looks like in around two and a half years it'll actually come pretty close to Earth . . . " Robert's voice lowered, "Jesus!" he said, examining the numbers again. "That's damn close," Robert said, watching Suri for a moment. "But it's not on a collision course. You're not telling me the plot of *Armageddon* are you?"

"It does come pretty close to Earth. It will pass between us and the Moon, actually. But that's not what worries me. If you look here . . . " Suri moved some windows around, showing the N-body simulation for planet orbital pathways. " . . . if we cross-correlate the optical data with the infrared, we can see the size and density of the comet. There's a gaseous pocket there, see it?"

"Yes, and?"

"Sir, combined with an average sublimation rate of the comet's surface," Suri continued unperturbed, and clicked another window open, "here is the corrected orbital path if we consider the effects of the gaseous plume."

Robert closed his eyes now, rubbing his temples, and looked up from the computer.

"Suri, you *are* telling me the plot of *Armageddon*, aren't you? You graduated MIT, correct?"

"Sir—"

"Computer science, if memory serves, with an emphasis on probability. So you know the extreme unlikeliness of such an event."

"I ran it three times, sir. Five sigma."

With that, Robert stopped. "What?"

"Five sigma."

The sigma refers to the probability that the calculation is the result of a random error or that the data is simply wrong. If the data is statistically significant to "five sigma," that means that there is a one-in-three-point-five-million chance that the data is incorrect. In other words, scientists *prove* things by labeling them "five sigma."

"My God."

"I'm pretty sure I did everything right, but I still could've made a mistake. In college, I messed up on a decimal point and disproved gravity before realizing I messed up."

Robert wasn't listening to Suri anymore.

"Suri, sit here and run it again. I'll do the same thing."

Together they sat and ran and reran the code, checking the numbers. They tested the accuracy of the initial reading under different astronomical circumstances, and went over their previous numbers to ensure they made no mistakes. Every single time, within two and a half years, the comet would hit

Earth. Dr. Miller was senior enough that when he logged in to the JSC supercomputer, he had the ability to log off everyone else. He did.

At around eleven a.m. there was a knock on the door.

"Go away," Robert mumbled.

The knock became more timid, but continued.

"Alright! Yes?"

A gangly, bespectacled, middle-aged man entered.

"What do you want, Brady?"

"You logged everyone out of Jarvis."

The supercomputer at NASA had been nicknamed Jarvis by Brady. He didn't have many friends.

"So what?"

"I was working on my—"

"Get out of here, Brady, before I crotch-punch you and give you a wedgie. I don't have time for your—"

He didn't even finish his thought before another person walked in, complaining about the supercomputer-hogging.

"Suri, please lock the door. Better yet, just stand out there and don't let anyone knock. Don't let me be disturbed. If anyone pushes you, push them back."

Suri gulped and got up to stand guard.

Robert felt a cold sweat on his forehead as he continued to check Suri's work. He had checked and rechecked and the math wasn't any different. At six forty-five p.m. he printed out the key pieces of Suri's discovery and burst through the door, almost knocking Suri over.

"Oh, sorry Suri, follow me. We have work to do."

They ran together through JSC to the Chief Scientist at NASA, Dr. Steven Goldberg. He had the corner office of corner offices, and they leapt in, despite the secretary's shrill admonishment.

"Goldberg!"

Dr. Goldberg sighed when he saw Robert.

"I was about to leave, Rob. What's going on that can't wait until Monday?"

"This," Robert said, thrusting the paper in front of NASA's Chief Scientist.

"Rob . . . I can't let you use Hubble or ALMA, especially since I've had people complaining all day about Jarvis—"

"You're using that stupid name for the computer too?" Robert asked, exasperated. "Whatever, it's not important—this is. Read it, Goldberg. We need to do this now. We need a visual confirmation."

"Confirmation of what?" Dr. Goldberg's furrowed brow turned to the paper on his desk. As he read, the furrow disappeared and a face replaced it that many would adopt in the coming months: the *oh-my-God-the-world's-going-to-end* face.

"Oy vey," Dr. Goldberg said, turning to his computer. "I'll grant you access. Where is the comet now?"

Robert gave him the coordinates, and with that, the years-long waitlist to use the telescopes were bypassed.

Within a few minutes the photos came on the screen, and they could see a tiny dot on a mostly black screen. When that small white dot showed up, Suri grimaced. Dr. Goldberg took off his glasses and rubbed his temples and breathed heavily. Robert shouted expletives at the top of his voice. They continued to look at the screen, and at that little white dot.

"Two and a half years," a hoarse Robert said.

Suri looked at her watch. It was seven p.m. Robert and Suri excused themselves from Dr. Goldberg's office and went back to work in Robert's, doing their best to learn as much about the comet as possible.

Four hours later, Suri looked at her watch again— eleven p.m. She dejectedly began packing her bag and mentioned it was much past her bedtime.

Robert looked at her. "Nonsense," he said. "We are getting a drink."

Dr. Goldberg poked his head into Robert's office. Everyone else had gone home, and they were the only ones still in the office. "I'm going home to kiss my wife. And pray. You two, make sure to be here by seven a.m. We have some calls to make."

Robert wasn't paying attention, so Suri

acknowledged NASA's Chief Scientist with a quick nod. Suri watched Dr. Goldberg walk back toward his office with his hand running anxiously through his curly hair.

"Sir, I . . . um . . . I'm not really a drinker."

"I think the fact that the world is about to end calls for at least one appletini, don't you?"

"Well, yes. I suppose it does."

2

JEREMY GENSER

February 22, 2016
Sam Houston High School

"Psh! Jer!"

Jeremy Genser looked to his right in Calculus class at his girlfriend Anna Chenko. She handed him a note. They had decided that instead of texting each other, they would hand notes to each other. Teachers were so obsessed with keeping kids off their phones that they were rarely caught. On the occasion they were, the teacher would look longingly on better days, say something about it being cute, and then the class would meander on as before.

Jasper's having a party tonight, want to go?

Jeremy looked over at Anna, then crumpled up

the piece of paper and fake-ate it, making Anna laugh.

"Jeremy!" A sharp cut went through him. Ms. Konig stared at him.

"Yes?" he responded, with a mouthful of paper.

"Are you eating in my class?"

"No."

"Finish whatever is in your mouth, swallow it, then pay attention. You may think this is not important, but if you want to be successful at MIT, you better pay attention, whether you think you know this material already or not."

Jeremy winked at Anna. She covered her mouth in disgust and admiration as Jeremy swallowed the disgusting ink-filled piece of paper. It tasted horrendous. He affected a smile while Ms. Konig smirked. She went over derivatives of sine and cosine again.

Once out of class, Anna smacked him on the arm.

"That was so gross, Jeremy. What is wrong with you?"

"I had to do it. She dared me."

"She didn't!"

"In her own way she did."

"Well, maybe. So what do you think about Jasper's?"

"Maybe. I told my Dad that I'd help him out at work, so if we finish quickly enough, I'll go."

"I'm counting that as a yes. Better not disappoint," Anna teased.

Jeremy and Anna kissed, and they went their separate ways—Anna to U.S. Government, and Jeremy to AP Biology. AP Biology was Jeremy's least favorite class because he knew nobody in it. He drifted in and out of paying attention, and one time he had to shake himself awake to keep himself from falling asleep.

"Jeremy!" Mr. Del Piero yelled. "Are you with us?"

"Yes, Mr. Del Piero," Jeremy replied, coming out of a deep daydream about those books like *The Lightning Thief* or *Harry Potter*, where the unsuspecting high school student is surprised to learn he actually possesses superpowers. Jeremy liked to pretend he was one of those guys.

"As I was saying," Mr. Del Piero mused, "the Cretaceous–Tertiary extinction occurred around sixty-six billion years ago. We know this event is what caused the extinction of the dinosaurs, but we don't know what exactly caused this event. The strongest evidence, however, is that there was a large impact event on the surface of the Earth that caused massive volcanic eruptions, tsunamis, and drastically changed the temperature of the Earth, which caused almost all prehistoric species to die. There are also other theories . . . "

Jeremy fell back asleep, unable to hold his eyelids up any longer. When the bell rang and Jeremy woke up, he happily realized it was fifth period, which meant that he had a ten-minute break. And since he had two free periods it was the end of his school day!

It was strange, there were only ten minutes in between classes, but somehow almost the entire school found the time to socialize. It had always fascinated Jeremy.

Jeremy walked past the Goths, the Jocks, the

Hipsters, the Stoners, the Rednecks, the Druggies, the Drama Kids, the Nerds, the Christians, the Muslims, and many more. Jeremy was a little in with the Nerds, the Jocks, and the Drama Kids. There wasn't a real "Cool Kids" group like in the movies, but Jeremy was cool by association from his girlfriend, Anna. Anna was the queen of the school. She was also the actual Homecoming Queen, which helped, but she had that *cool* aura about her—the kind of contagious kindness that is usually absent from the beautiful people of the world. She had won two genetic lotteries—brains and looks. Some of her friendliness leaked off on Jeremy, as boyfriend to the Queen, but he was much too nerdy to truly be one of the cool kids. His best friend, Dustin, was a Drama Kid, which automatically made him weird and crazy. Dustin was a true friend, loyal to the last lion.

As if on cue, Dustin walked over and fist-bumped Jeremy.

"She's pretty cute, huh?" Dustin said, motioning

at Karina, a girl in their grade who was friends with Anna.

"Yeah, I guess," Jeremy answered.

"See you at the party tonight?"

"I don't know. I have to work."

"Then come after, it's not like there's anything going on on Tuesday anyway."

"Good point," Jeremy replied.

They fist-bumped again, and in a flash Dustin ran over to Karina, who sat with a few friends under an oak tree.

Jeremy walked down the steps out of the school, then to the parking lot, where he pulled out his lanyard. He swung it from his fingers.

Jeremy was almost six feet tall, and his doctor said he'd get to six-foot-two. He couldn't wait for that. He privately hoped it would happen before basketball season, but knew in his mind that it wouldn't. He climbed into his Subaru Outback (which definitely downgraded his *cool*) and began to get excited. He had been waiting for this for an entire week.

Jeremy's father, Earl Genser, was a well-established independent contractor in the Houston area, and a month ago he had secured perhaps the biggest job of his career. Genser Lighting specialized in commercial lighting systems, but without that "hospital" feel. Jeremy's dad had let his son work on the electrical systems since he was a boy, and Jeremy had gotten more than a few nasty shocks from it. Nevertheless, he'd always enjoyed the work. Because of his father's tutelage, Jeremy had been admitted to the Massachusetts Institute of Technology, the Holy Mecca for Nerds.

Jeremy raced home, excited to work for his father.

"Hey, Jay," his father said when he opened the front door. "It's a big day today, and since you are now eighteen, I have a surprise for you."

"Is it a new car?"

Earl laughed while folding up the newspaper he was reading. "Wishful thinking, son. But, I have decided to pay you the standard hourly rate for your services. Now that you are of age, and have proven yourself a good lighting contractor, I will let you work for standard pay, instead of the usual pay."

Jeremy smirked. "Usual pay? You don't ever pay me anything!"

"As I have always said: room and board. You've been living under my roof for eighteen years and—"

"Yeah, yeah, Dad. I know."

Earl laughed boisterously. He was not a skinny man, nor a tall one. Jeremy guessed he got his height from his mother, a black-haired woman of six-foot-one.

"Well, Jay," Earl put an arm around Jeremy, "now you become a man."

Jeremy had thought he was a man long before his father told him, but then again he was pretty sure most eighteen-year-old boys thought the same thing. Jeremy hopped into his father's Dodge Ram and they sped off into the Houston traffic for the Johnson Space Center.

• • •

Jeremy walked around the glorious main lobby in awe, even though the JSC had seen better days. Private competition from companies like SpaceX and Blue Origin were threatening NASA, but it still held much of its former glory. There were odes to NASA's various missions, like a scale model of *Columbia*, the command module of the Apollo 11 mission, the first manned ship to the Moon. Scientists were everywhere, all looking on their phones or speaking into them or reading from pieces of paper. It was amazing they didn't all run into each other. Maybe the scientists had eyes in the backs of their heads, or maybe on top would be more appropriate, since so many heads were bent down to their phones.

Jeremy was put to work immediately by his father, who put him in charge of the most onerous part of the job: climbing into the attic area above the ceiling and running the wiring to and from each lighting fixture.

"Why me, Dad?"

"Because you are skinny as a twig, Jer, and none

of my guys can fit as comfortably as you." Another boisterous laugh came from Earl.

Jeremy sighed. At least he would get to watch scientists from above. Maybe he would even try to scare a few. He tried whispering, "God is watching," to a few passing underneath, but he didn't speak loud enough for them to hear him.

Jeremy was still stuck in the ceiling at around six p.m. when his father called up to him.

"Alright Jeremy, good work today. I'm impressed!"

"Thanks, Dad!"

"Come down and we'll go grab some burritos before we head home."

"Sounds good."

With that, Jeremy climbed down from the thin ceiling and stepped precariously onto the ladder. Suddenly three scientists, two men and a trailing woman, ran past the ladder. The sudden gust almost caused Jeremy to fall, and his father yelled, "Hey, watch it!" The scientists paid no attention. In fact, it looked like they hadn't noticed anything at all.

"That was weird," Jeremy said as he stepped back down on the ground.

"Engineers. They aren't really good with people," Earl said, putting his arm around his son, "That's why you're going to do so great at MIT, Jeremy. You know how to talk to people."

As with all of his father's compliments, he could only say thank you and try not to get red in the face, which of course he did anyway.

They drove up the Gulf Freeway and stopped off at Rodrigo's, a Mexican restaurant known for its spectacular burritos. Jeremy wolfed down his burrito like only a teenage boy can (under thirty-nine seconds was his record without vomiting). Then he drove home and showered as quickly as possible before heading out for the night.

3

PROJECT MARS

February 22, 2016
Southeast Houston

Suri looked at herself in her bathroom mirror, thinking about what she should wear. Normally it didn't take her this long, but today was an important day. The Secretary of State, Nicholas Brighton, would touch down in Houston in under two hours. It was her job, along with Robert and Dr. Goldberg, to brief him on the comet they had found, Comet J312. After that, they would have a video call with the President of the United States, Victoria Chaplin. Just two years ago, Suri was a senior at the Massachusetts Institute of Technology, living in Boston, and very much ignorant of what she should do with her life. Now she was about to meet Nicholas Brighton and—albeit virtually—the President of the United States.

This made her very anxious, and she looked through her supply of clothes for the right pant-suit. Her normal clothes choice of jeans and a geeky T-Shirt would be a bit informal, so she really only had a couple of options. She dug in the back of her closet to find something respectable, settling on gray pleated pants, a white blouse, and a matching gray blazer.

She decided not to make lunch, and coffee was out of the question, since her heart was already beating out of her chest. Taylor Swift was playing on the radio: "Bad Blood." Her heart didn't stop beating fast even when she sat in the typical Houston traffic, listening to Taylor's melodic voice coupled with the angry car horns outside.

Robert had told her to meet him in his office when she arrived on Monday, and they would go over their brief before the Secretary of State arrived. The JSC looked a bit different than when she had left it on Friday. There were more security guards, and people with earpieces and expensive-looking suits were stationed everywhere. They spoke in hushed tones and stood stoically.

"Good morning," Suri said when she walked into Robert's office.

"Suri, good morning. Your work on the comet was very well done. I am impressed."

Robert looked like he hadn't showered since Friday. His white hair was even more unkempt than usual, and papers were strewn all around his desk.

"Are you ready for the presentation?" he asked.

"Yes," Suri said nervously. Even thinking about having to speak publicly made her feel nauseous. She continued, "Do you think maybe you could do my part of the presentation? I mean, I'm not too comf—"

"No. You will do it."

The finality with which Robert spoke made Suri smile and for some reason made her a little less nervous.

"Okay."

"Suri, you're competent, you are a decent communicator, and most of all, you are smart. We are dealing with professional politicians here. You're much smarter than them. We just have to get them to understand that we need money to do our jobs. From now until twenty-eight months from now, we have a new job: save the world."

"I don't think you're helping my anxiety, sir . . . " Suri stammered, but Robert ignored her.

"Kind of exciting, isn't it? We, right now, have the ability and the skills to save the entire world. It's not often that the work of astrophysicists is life-and-death. It actually never is, except now. Now all we need is someone to believe in us. Just think of it as that. Some people are coming, and they want to give us money."

"Um, okay."

"They just also happen to be the leaders of the free world!" Robert exclaimed.

"Now you're definitely not helping." Suri grimaced.

At that moment, one of the expensive-looking suits walked in the door, mentioned that they were due to be in the general conference room in ten minutes, and walked out. After a little more preparation, Suri and Robert headed out.

Suri watched Robert walk purposefully under a construction ladder on the way. A balding contractor standing on the penultimate step swore at him for jostling the ladder.

"You know that's bad luck!" Dr. Goldberg, NASA's Chief Scientist, called. Dr. Goldberg was a few paces behind them as he tried to catch up.

"Any luck is good luck," Robert replied.

"Don't they always tell you to imagine everyone naked in the crowd, to make public speaking easier?" Suri wondered aloud, trying not to freak out.

"If it helps," Dr. Goldberg said, smiling.

Robert was a man on a mission. He had not felt this alive in a long while, though it felt now that he alternated between aggressively attacking the end of the world, and finding it hopeless. He spent the better part of Friday night and Saturday morning drinking himself into a stupor, but on Sunday he had awoken with a fire in him. He had spent long hours devising a strategy. Walking under the ladder was just a personal "screw you" to God. *We won't let bad luck stand in our way. Not even a comet can stop the human race. We will overcome,* he thought. *We must.*

He walked into the conference room, Suri in tow. Everyone was already inside, and stood up to greet him. The Public Relations rep, Daniel Atkins, nodded his hello. Various other heads of NASA's different departments nodded as well. The Director of NASA, Nate Goodrich, stared solemnly at Robert, as if he was somehow far away from the crisis.

Directly in front of Nate stood the "cash cows"— the people Robert would have to win over. Nicholas Brighton, the Secretary of State, looked intimidating. He was six feet tall, but seemed to take up the whole room with his aura. He was fit, and though his black hair was graying, he still looked like he would play basketball with the best of them. His bodyguards stared, unblinking, directly forward.

On the television screen sat many people Robert recognized but had never paid much attention to. Among them were: the White House Press Secretary, the Speaker of the House, six members of the president's Cabinet, and the Chairman of the Joint Chiefs of Staff, General Diaz.

"Please be seated," said Secretary Brighton. Everyone took his or her seat, Suri sitting next to Robert around a big conference table.

NASA Director Nate Goodrich spoke up in a detached tone. "Allow me to introduce Dr. Robert Miller, director of the Astrophysics Department. He is leading a team of astrophysicists who specialize in looking at the farthest reaches of our solar system."

Secretary Brighton shook Robert's hand and said, "Nice to meet you, Dr. Miller. Thank you for taking the time to meet with us. Who is this with you?"

Secretary Brighton asked. "Director Goodrich failed to introduce her."

"Ah, yes. This is Dr. Suri Lahdka. She has been working alongside me in our department, and has been working specifically for Kuiper Search 15439. She found the comet first."

"Hello, Mr. Secretary," Suri said.

"It's nice to meet you, Doctor. I, on behalf of the United States of America, would like to thank you for your service to NASA."

Robert noticed there was a person who was very obviously not present at the meeting: The president, Victoria Chaplin.

"Where is President Chaplin?" he asked.

"She is in a meeting with the Prime Minister of Australia, and it would have been irresponsible to cancel it last minute. We will fill her in. Please begin," Secretary Brighton responded.

A little deflated, Robert got out his computer, hooked it up to the projector, and set up his presentation catered specifically for the politicians. The first slide came up with some preliminary statistics, and Robert began his rehearsed speech.

"As of Friday morning, Dr. Suri Lahdka found a previously undiscovered comet, Comet J312, in the Kuiper belt, a region of the solar system beyond the orbit of Neptune. We believe that some time ago, this comet came into contact with a large cosmic body, which altered its orbit. When we discovered it on Friday and ran our model to determine its new orbit, we found it is on a deadly collision path with Earth." He paused. "Due to its size, it is capable of exterminating all life on our planet."

Robert looked up, expecting to see a room full of the *oh-my-god-we-are-all-going-to-die* faces. Several people swore under their breaths, but the politicians either had already done their gasps or they were used to dealing with literally "Earth-shattering" news. A few of the NASA employees gasped and covered their mouths. The Public Relations rep, Daniel Atkins, yelped out loud.

"The comet is around forty kilometers in

diameter, or twenty-four-point-nine miles. This is an extinction-size comet. All life on Earth will be destroyed, aside from perhaps small microbes living in sedimentary rocks, and organisms living near or under the ocean floor perhaps. Certainly, all of humanity will be wiped off the face of the Earth, within seconds of impact."

Robert looked back at Suri and exhaled, and the Secretary of State finished scribbling on his notepad. Again, Robert thought the politicians should be turning pale from the news.

"Where exactly did this meteor come from? Was it just shooting through space and came into our solar system?" Secretary Brighton asked.

Robert looked over at Suri, who briefly felt her heart jump into her throat. She swallowed it back down, and answered. "So the meteor . . . Well, first of all, it isn't really a meteor. It's a comet. A meteor is what we call a shooting star. It's the light phenomenon we see in the sky. A comet is a relatively small icy body in space, which is what we are dealing with.

Anyway, outside of the solar system is basically empty space, so everything close enough to the Sun ends up orbiting the Sun. So, past Neptune, around the same distance away from the Sun as Pluto, there are a lot of comets in the area known as the Kuiper Belt. So, what probably happened, is that this comet, Comet J312, collided with another comet which drastically changed its orbit. We are lucky to have found it at all—comets are hard to spot. Anyway, when Earth reaches its perihelion—the point when it's closest to the Sun—Comet J312 will hit Earth."

At this point Suri clicked the PowerPoint through to a slide containing a graphic showing a small comet hurtling toward the inner part of the solar system.

"As J312 gets closer to the Sun, it will get smaller because the Sun will sublimate it—turn the ices into gases. Since its outer layers have different compositions, they will sublimate at different speeds, which will make the comet's path move. Inside this comet, a pocket below the surface contains a large amount of gaseous ammonia. When the Sun melts the outer layer, the ammonia will shoot out, causing it to act as a sort of jet—"

"So it might not hit us? We don't really know yet what its exact trajectory is, right?" Public Relations Daniel Atkins asked optimistically.

"Well, no—" Suri began.

Dr. Miller jumped in. "Daniel, while it is true that it may not hit us, it is extremely likely that it will. Based on our calculations I'm comfortable telling you—off the record—that it is ninety-nine-point-nine percent likely to hit Earth. Let's plan for this impact, so that if it does our species won't be exterminated."

Everyone nodded in agreement, and one of the politicians asked, "And how exactly did you find this comet?"

"I found it when Dr. Miller gave me the project of going through the LSST's most recent photographs and data dump."

"Would you mind explaining this, please?" General Diaz cut in with his rough voice.

"Um, sure," Suri answered. "So the LSST, or Large Sky Survey Telescope, is a very expensive telescope that takes pictures of the sky. Every night it takes dozens of photos, along with all sorts of data to sort through. Basically, different research teams will lobby for different parts of the sky to be photographed. So we take the pictures, and then anyone can use the information—it's open source. So the photos taken on December 4th, 2015, of a region in between the orbits of Uranus and Neptune, were originally asked for by a Russian research team.

"Dr. Miller gave me the task of checking this data, which is something I do a lot here. Once I crunched the numbers, I spotted an abnormally large and very dark comet coming toward the Sun, at a relatively fast speed. After some very preliminary modeling, we found the collision date. We confirmed this using three different telescopes."

The Secretary of State stopped Suri with a question. "This data that you looked through, did the Russians give it to you?"

"Um, no, Dr. Miller did," Suri replied.

Dr. Miller realized what the Secretary was getting at. He was wondering if the data was faulty and if the Russians were using this comet as a diversion for something. Robert answered the question. "The data is open source, which means anyone can view and download it. Once the LSST takes the photos, scientists from all over the world have access. The data is protected from tampering, so there's no chance that Russia altered it."

At this point, Secretary of State Brighton spoke up. "The president has asked us to freeze this data to anyone who hasn't already downloaded it. We have already done this. As of two hours ago the data you now possess, along with access to the LSST satellite, is your own. PR will figure out something to tell the other nations and scientists to explain why the data is no longer open source."

"Wait a minute!" Robert said. "You want to keep them in the dark?"

"It's a matter of national security," Secretary Brighton said.

"But—" Robert thought of his plan to include other top scientists in his team.

"You'll have complete access to all data for anything related to Comet J312."

"I don't need more data! I need every single intelligent mind we've got—especially the astronomers," Robert interjected angrily. "This includes those from other nations. They may have ideas that could save the world!"

"Dr. Miller, it is of utmost importance that we maintain order. If the public were to know that the world may very well end within the next three years, who would follow laws? Who would pay the taxes we'll need to pay for this project? For now, we must keep them in the dark. This is of paramount importance to our survival. We might have a bona fide two and a half year countdown, but do not underestimate the power of chaos and fear. If we let this go to the public now, our clock may expire much sooner."

So, they want to keep it all a secret, Robert thought angrily. *We'll see how long that lasts.* Dr. Miller turned his attention back to Suri, who was waiting to continue.

Suri clicked to the next slide of her PowerPoint. "One thing we are working on is predicting how the comet's trajectory will change as it melts. This, coupled with Dr. Miller's plan to move the comet out of our orbit, may give us a chance at survival." She turned to Dr. Miller and sat down.

Dr. Miller leveled his eyes at the politicians on the screen. "Moving the comet may require the use of nuclear weapons. I suggest that we start centrifuging as much plutonium as we can in order to prepare. I also ask for the top nuclear physicists to be relocated to Houston so they can work with us."

"Dr. Miller," General Diaz said, stiffening, "we will begin production of whatever hardware you need. But plutonium production will bring instability. What is to stop other nations proliferating their own nuclear weapons capabilities when they see we are strengthening ours?"

"Chairman Diaz," Robert responded, "like it or not, nuclear bombs may be our most successful weapon against the comet. This endeavor will go beyond our international borders; this must be a global effort to halt something that doesn't just threaten democracy, or freedom. It threatens the entire human race."

"It's *General* Diaz," General Diaz corrected, before adding, "So nuclear weapons are the leading strategy?"

"For now, yes," Robert answered.

"And how do you plan on deploying them?"

"We will design rockets that can deploy them at the comet. This is new territory for all scientists, and something we have never tried to do before," Suri added.

"Do you think it can work?" Secretary Brighton asked.

"It's possible, but we can't do it in the dark," Robert responded.

"I understand your point," the Secretary explained, "but for now, let's keep this information secure. In the meantime, make a list of your top scientists—your dream team, if you will. We'll use our channels of diplomacy to recruit them and bring them here to JSC. For now, JSC will be our base of operations.

"This project will go under the name Project Mars. Since we have to publish our budget we can use a cover about a project to send astronauts to Mars. There is already a team of Secret Service agents and Army and Marine forces dedicated to ensuring the security of Project Mars. You can imagine how crazy our country will become if people realize it very well may end in less than three years."

The Secretary straightened his tie. "This is not a threat. But consider: our country has always been one where freedom and democracy thrive, but we also have a strong streak of individualism that may hamper the effectiveness of everyone to stop an extinction-level event from occurring. Imagine what a countdown clock might do to the Rule of Law. That is where you come in, Mr. Atkins."

"Yes, sir," Daniel said while composing himself.

"That goes for all of you. You cannot speak to anyone about your work here. You are working on a new mission to reassert our dominance of the last frontier—space. Obviously secrecy is best, but to your family and close friends, you will be working to put a man on Mars. I understand that eventually the truth will come out—it always does, but the longer we can work silently, diligently, and purposefully, the more of a chance we have. This is a matter of global security. Do not speak of this to anyone."

After looking around the room to ensure everyone would follow his guidelines of secrecy, Secretary Brighton added, "Now, I believe we have another issue to address." He turned to Director Goodrich. "You have failed. Explain to us why Russia told us of the comet a full two weeks ago and you did nothing."

"Sir, I didn't think—" Director Goodrich began.

"What?!" Dr. Miller exclaimed angrily, cutting the director off. He looked mad enough to have steam coming from his ears. "We've wasted two weeks of work because you didn't want to tell anyone?"

Robert fumed at the ashamed NASA director. Suri was surprised he wasn't swearing yet.

"Well . . . " The Secretary of State looked contemptuously at the NASA director before continuing. " . . . it's time for us to get on the same page, then. We've known about the meteor for two weeks. Russian intelligence sent us the information."

"Comet . . . " Suri muttered, but no one heard her.

"I can't believe this—" Robert began a tirade of curses.

Oh well, Suri thought, *so much for no swearing.*

The Secretary continued unperturbed. "We gave the go-ahead to Director Goodrich to share this information with a specialized task force last week, but evidently he has become a bit depressed, and found no reason to begin an effort to save the planet."

"It's hopeless . . . forty kilometers across . . . " The director admitted, rubbing his eyes.

"Coward," Robert said.

"I couldn't agree more, Dr. Miller. What we need now are people, like you and Dr. Lahdka, who will fight to the last second against this inanimate foe. You will, I assume, fight?"

Dr. Miller, who was never a very patriotic person, stood up straight then, standing to attention for the Secretary. "Yes, I will."

He looked at Suri, who swallowed hard and said, "Yes, I will."

"Excellent. Well, then, let's get to work. Secretary of Energy Mahoney, start on the plutonium, and I will speak to you in two weeks about the progress. Spare no expense. Now, for our communication . . . " A bald Secret Service agent stepped forward, unsmiling, and began to hand out small boxes to everyone at the table, and Secretary Brighton continued, "These are end-to-end encrypted phones. Dr. Miller, here are five phones—one for yourself, and four for the rest of your team—and flash drives with all the information Russia gave us regarding the comet. I will be your official liaison with the White House, but understand I also have to be running our foreign policy.

"We will speak soon, and I expect a report of what you are doing in seven days. Meanwhile, I will schedule a visit to JSC by the president. Don't worry, she is not nearly as dominating in real life as she was in those debates."

Secretary Brighton exhaled a deep sigh. "This meeting is adjourned. May God be with you."

4

THE KIDS HAVE A PLAN

March 21, 2016
The Gulf Freeway, south of Houston

Jeremy drove toward Anna's house for dinner. He had been working at the JSC with his father for four weeks, and even though his father still had him doing the dirty work, he was enjoying it greatly. Right after school from Monday to Wednesday he would work for a few hours with his father, making money and getting experience in the real world. He rapidly learned it was much different than school.

The lighting project his dad had him working on was a great success. It was such a big success, in fact, that they asked him to retrofit another wing of the JSC as well. Jeremy asked if this would mean he would get a raise.

His father thought this was very funny.

"Yeah, when pigs fly, Jer," he said, but after work one day he gave Jeremy an extra hundred dollar bill, winking as he did.

Jeremy had only two true anxieties about his life: one, how his basketball team would do this season—they had been projected as one of the best teams in their division—and two, his girlfriend Anna's questions about their relationship after high school. Anna had a tendency to think too far in advance, and sometimes this made Jeremy's job of living in the present more difficult. Now, however, he had a new worry. Lately, at the JSC, Jeremy had noticed something strange going on. He had decided to talk to Anna about it. Maybe she would tell him that he was just being paranoid.

Dinner with Anna's family was nice. They were a very traditional and conservative family. It made Anna stand out, since she had a nose piercing and dark red hair, compared with her blonde family. She dyed her hair that way, and Jeremy thought it looked good—almost more natural than the blonde hair she used to have. Her father worked for an oil company, one of the biggest in Houston, which accounted for their remarkable wealth.

After dinner, Jeremy finally had the chance to tell Anna about his suspicions about the JSC. Anna lived in River Oaks, which was one of the nicest residential areas in Houston, so they went for a walk among the large Victorian and French-style mansions.

Anna was talking about something but Jeremy had trouble paying attention. Finally, he interrupted her:

"Something weird is going on at the Johnson Space Center."

"What do you mean?" Anna asked with wide eyes, as they walked by the nicely cut lawns and impeccable rose bushes.

"I don't know. It's probably nothing." Jeremy replied, losing confidence. He'd been at the JSC for over a month, crawling around the ceiling, climbing ladders near top-secret conversations, and fetching tools for his father, so the place had started to look familiar. He started noticing changes happening at the JSC that just didn't make sense to him.

"Come on, even if it's nothing, just tell me. You brought it up for a reason, right?" Anna said, a little annoyed.

"Well, okay. I'm probably crazy, but lately I've noticed so many security guards there, and they all are dressed in really nice suits, and they all have earpieces."

"Maybe the president is going to visit?" Anna mused.

Jeremy frowned. "Could be, but it's been a month and the security is only increasing. Wouldn't the president have come and gone by now? And yesterday . . . well, I spend a lot of time in the ceiling, running lighting fixtures, and the main hub of wiring is above this small closet. I've caught like ten people crying in that closet! At first I thought it was just a bad breakup or something, because a girl was tapping her phone over and over again, but the next day, it was a different girl. And then two guys, crying together!"

"A crying closet," Anna mused. "That is weird."

"And today a bunch of foreign scientists showed up. I even looked some of them up. Five of them are Russian nuclear physicists."

"Whoa. That's weird. I thought Russia and the U.S. didn't get along, especially with nuclear stuff," Anna commented.

"Yeah, it's weird . . . " Jeremy rubbed his chin as a posh woman strolled by walking a Pomeranian.

When the woman was out of earshot, Jeremy asked, "Do you want to help me find out what's going on? It could be nothing, but it would be fun!"

"You mean an adventure?" Anna frowned. "You're asking me out on an adventure date, aren't you?"

"Yes."

"Of course!" Anna slung her arms around Jeremy's neck, hugging him.

"Great, I'll pick you up tomorrow after school!"

"Wait," Anna pouted.

Jeremy had already turned, ready to walk Anna back home.

"You always do that."

"Do what?" Jeremy asked.

"You never tell me what we're going to do! Tell me!"

"That's because I'm not quite sure yet." He needed to consult his partner in crime: Dustin.

Anna gave him one of her scowls, but there was a glint of mischief in her eye.

They turned the corner of Anna's street and Jeremy's parked car came into view. After kissing Anna goodnight, Jeremy hopped in and sped off toward Dustin's house. On the way he thought about all the odd things he had seen at the JSC, especially in the past week. The increased security was definitely the biggest factor. He saw workers unloading those mysterious government SUVs almost daily. One time, one of the workers dropped a box—they were big black boxes that looked extremely heavy. When it dropped, Jeremy saw it was full of black binders labeled *Top Secret.*

After they cleaned everything up, Jeremy followed the boxes to an area in the JSC he hadn't been to before, but when he tried to peek into the room where the workers were headed, he got blocked.

"There's no access here."

"But I'm a—"

The military grunt didn't move a muscle and folded his arms, and Jeremy figured it was useless to argue.

He snapped out of his reverie, parked his car, and walked behind Dustin's house, scaled onto the roof of the garage, and tapped on the window to Dustin's room.

Dustin sat in his chair, pleasantly surprised by the arrival of his friend, opening the window, and greeting him. He sat back and listened to Jeremy intently.

"So this scientist, Dr. Miller," Jeremy began, "he has a nice office, and it's a nice corner office, you know. It has a view of the lawn and stuff at the JSC,

61

but the layout isn't huge. It's not like the NASA director's office, which is huge and elegant. Even the door is unassuming. All it says is: 'Dr. Miller, Director of Astrophysics and Kuiper Belt Research.' Aside from that, it looks like any other door. But it's literally the center of all the JSC. It's where everyone comes from, and goes to."

"Maybe he has some project that requires everyone?" Dustin asked.

"Maybe, but there's literally always a line of people outside the door, and when he leaves his room, the whole line follows him!"

"He's like Justin Bieber and they are like a bunch of teenage girls! Has he made any pop hits?" Dustin joked.

"Dustin, this is serious. I want to hack into his email address," Jeremy stated flatly, making Dustin's gaze become serious.

"You want to hack into a government scientist's email account?" Dustin asked, aghast, until he couldn't help but grin. He loved a challenge, even if it meant getting in trouble.

"Yes."

"Wow . . . " Dustin looked shrewdly at his friend.

Jeremy told him more about the odd behavior at NASA the past few weeks.

"What do you think they are doing?" Dustin asked, slowly becoming more curious.

"I don't know! They found water on Mars recently, right? Maybe it's something to do with that?"

"Maybe they found life!"

"Yeah, that would be so cool. I bet we would get an A for sure in Physics if we showed the class there was proof of life on Mars!"

They laughed, and Dustin began explaining how hacking an email might work.

"Well, there's lots of ways to do this. One way is to install a program on the scientist's computer called a 'keylogger.' That would keep track of all the keystrokes on his computer—of all the keys he hits.

We'd have to physically log in to his computer first, though, and then install the program. Then we could have the keystrokes sent to us, and we could figure out all his passwords—"

"But then we'd still have to be in his office, right? Is there any way to do this remotely?" Jeremy interrupted.

"Well, I'd need an hour with my computer while logged into the JSC servers, which would be risky. Even if they don't catch me, they'll see everything I've done. So when we leave, the government will go straight to our houses."

"Good thing we are only seventeen, so they can't send us to jail," Jeremy joked, but Dustin didn't find it funny.

"We would need to use someone else's computer that has no connection to us."

"And you'd need an hour to hack into it?"

"Yeah, around an hour. We only want to look at his emails and documents, so it shouldn't be too hard. I could even download them onto a flash drive for us to look at later." Dustin furrowed his brow, thinking. "But all of this sounds a little hard to do. I think, since the JSC—and all internet stuff—is being so tightly protected, it might be better to just go at it the old fashioned way."

Jeremy looked at Dustin sideways. "What do you mean? We have all this technology, and you don't want to use it?"

"Exactly!" Dustin replied triumphantly. "People can track all that stuff now. That's how they knew it was China and Russia hacking into the U.S. government. They couldn't do anything about it because it's China and Russia, but they could definitely do some bad stuff to us. But, let's say that we distract Dr. Miller for a second in a hallway or something, and unplug the cameras, and just run into his room, steal some papers or look at some stuff on his computer—maybe take some photos. If we get caught, we act like stupid innocent kids, and they don't have any real evidence against us anyway."

"So you're saying act like stupid teenagers because that's what everyone thinks we are?"

"Exactly . . . " Dustin replied.

Jeremy didn't tell Dustin that Anna had already agreed to help—and he liked Dustin's plan. They went over everything three times to make sure they had it down, and agreed to meet after school.

●　●　●

Robert's workload had increased to at least ninety hours a week. He was always working, or thinking about work. Rarely did the comet wander from his mind, and when it did he oddly found himself wondering what Elise, his ex-wife, was up to. Once upon a time, just after Robert had gotten his PhD, he'd fallen in love with a woman named Elise, who worked at his favorite coffee shop. They had a daughter, Jennifer, but things had moved too fast for them both, plus a million other clichés, and they split up when Jennifer was young. Since the comet had taken over Robert's life, it was Jennifer and Elise that took his mind hostage. Robert and Elise had cut contact long ago, and Jennifer was now probably an adult. Even though he didn't have a Facebook account, he was sure they would be on there, so he had entertained looking them up on the internet.

He had even called Jennifer a few times, but always hung up the phone before she answered. What would he say? "Hi honey, I know it has been a while, but the world is about to end, and I want to be with you before it does. But I'll be working so much you'll probably never see me. How does that sound?" He was sure she would think he was crazy.

His time was filled with managing the now hundreds of people working under him. Luckily, he had Suri, who turned out to be enormously helpful. Even though she was fresh from her post-doctorate, she knew a lot more than he did when he was her age.

Robert had set up another office desk and chair for Suri in his office so they could work together, but pretty soon they would have to move. He had heard that contractors were converting a big conference room for them, so they could work together on these projects. It was going to take a lot of work. Only three weeks had passed since what Robert liked to call "D-Day," or "Discovery Day"—the day Suri walked into his office to tell him the news.

Already, Robert had flown in several nuclear physicists from Russia to help. He had also tasked the Jet Propulsion Laboratory in Pasadena, California with building rockets equipped with multiple thrusters capable of 360° movement. They would need it in order to maneuver the nuclear-equipped rockets to hit the unpredictable comet. He had nicknamed the comet Shiva. Goldberg wanted to go with Jesus, or another biblical reference, but Robert liked Shiva. When Suri read Robert's choice of nickname for the comet, she briskly walked over to her superior's office.

"Shiva? You really named the comet Shiva?" she asked crossly.

"Destroyer of Worlds," Robert answered, not looking up from his computer. "I thought it fit."

"This doesn't have anything to do with the fact that I'm Indian, and I found the comet?" Suri asked again, perturbed by the use of Hinduism's most feared gods.

"Shiva was the name J. Robert Oppenheimer gave himself when he built the first atomic bomb. It's only fitting that we might save the world with his bombs from a destructive comet called Shiva . . . right?"

Suri thought about this for a second, and then she walked out of the office, unable to decide whether the name was perfect or offensive.

The data had been public for a few weeks before the United States and Russia took it offline. Several scientists had sent angry emails demanding that data. The scientists cried that this was against the core tenets of the scientific community, which was true. The data that the satellite spat out was open source, meaning anyone could read it. But since the world would have a colossal freak-out if it knew the world was going to end, they decided to shut it down. The only countries that had begun downloading and using the information were Chile, Russia, and the United States, and this was sheer luck that it was only three countries. The Chilean scientists who were working on the data had called Dr. Miller a week ago, and now they were working at JSC as well, along with many others from Robert's hand-picked list. The Chilean government, however, had not agreed to keep things silent.

• • •

"Got it?" Jeremy asked.

"Are you crazy?!" Anna asked, appalled.

"What?" Jeremy said, innocently.

"We'll go to jail! We won't go to college. We—"

"Listen, you don't have to do this if you don't want to. I can have Dustin help me. And if we get caught, we just act stupid. The worst case scenario is that our parents ground us. But, I think, NASA is getting ready to do something . . . big . . . something scary—"

Now it was Anna's turn to interrupt him. "You can't just wait for them to tell the whole world like a normal person?"

Jeremy thought for a second, then he said, "No. I can't. I want to know now. Don't you?"

"Not really."

"Come on," Jeremy teased, pleading with her. "It'll be fun. Consider it a test of your acting skills."

"Not fair," Anna replied. Jeremy knew his girl-friend's weakness for challenges.

"Nothing bad will happen, and even if it does, and we get caught, we are just some stupid naïve high schoolers with a thirst for knowledge."

Anna looked over to Jeremy in the driver seat and narrowed her eyes at him. It was true that the worst case scenario would be that they get yelled at for being impulsive. But what if the consequences were more serious? Mr. Genser could probably bail them out, Anna thought. Reluctantly, but with little excited butterflies in her stomach, she agreed to help.

Before they made the turn onto Saturn Lane, Jeremy stopped on the side of the road. Since Anna didn't have a contractor's badge to the JSC, she got out and climbed into the trunk.

"Don't accelerate too fast!" she said.

Dustin would stay at home, monitoring their locations using their cell phones through an end-to-end encrypted group chat.

Jeremy drove nervously through the gates of JSC. *Better to ask for forgiveness than permission*, he thought.

By now, the security guards recognized Jeremy's car and his badge, and waved him through the gate without question. He parked in the employee lot, and, careful to make sure nobody saw him, popped the trunk. Anna quickly stepped out and smoothed her clothes. She wore tight jeans, boots, and a shirt with a deep V-neck. Jeremy wore jeans and a white T-shirt—his typical work clothes.

Anna and Jeremy walked up together through the JSC lobby and down the hallway to Dr. Miller's office. They watched as people shuffled in and out; it was hardly ever unoccupied. The door was never left open, so it was difficult to hear conversations inside. Jeremy could swear he heard something about Mars, but it could have been about *stars* or *cars* too. Anna busied herself outside Dr. Miller's office by setting up the ladder and beginning to dismantle the ceiling panels above the hallway.

Jeremy walked into the supply closet in the hallway near Dr. Miller's office and looked up. The characteristic foam ceiling panels loomed above him. He found a stool, climbed onto it, and moved one of the tiles, settling in between the structural ceiling and the false one that so many office buildings used. He climbed across the precarious ceiling, making sure not to fall. Jeremy checked his phone's compass to make sure he was going the right way.

Before long he was directly over Dr. Miller's office. There, as silently as he could, he moved one of the panels just enough to clearly see the door and much of the room.

He texted I'm in to Dustin and Anna.

At this point, the trap was set, and very simple. Anna would dismantle the ceiling panels and place wires just outside of Dr. Miller's office. When Dr. Miller left and there was no one in the room, Jeremy would jump down from the ceiling and take photos of everything he could. Then he'd send the photos in the encrypted group chat, and fix the ceiling panel before walking out the front door to continue working.

Dr. Miller, however, stayed put in his chair. Jeremy crouched uncomfortably in his position, watching Dr. Miller type away on his computer. His knees began to hurt and his muscles cramped. Every once in a while Dr. Miller would yawn, which Jeremy began to find legitimately exciting compared to watching nothing.

This is so boring, Jeremy texted after an hour of waiting.

I thought you said he gets a bunch of visitors all the time and is always moving around? Anna texted.

Jeremy: I guess not now . . .

Anna: Grrr. Well I'm going to start measuring the walls' dimensions.

I'm watching House of Cards! Dustin replied.

After another fifteen minutes, Jeremy heard a knock at the door.

Dr. Miller, who had said nothing but the occasional *hmph* for the past ninety minutes, spoke up.

"Yes," he said.

A petite woman entered.

"The numbers for the initial model are in. The emission jets can be catalyzed by us. In order to intercept, we have one month to launch a bomb," she said.

"Will we have flight control throughout?"

"Under this model, yes."

"Okay, I'll send it over to JPL and tell them the timeline. How big of a bomb do we need?"

"Forty-five kilotons."

"Okay. Thanks, Suri."

Jeremy held his breath as he listened to the two scientists speak. *What the heck is going on?* he thought. *Kilotons . . . that sounds like an atomic bomb. Are we starting another war?*

"You're still there," Robert mumbled.

Jeremy tried to lean in closer, trying to hear.

" . . . I just . . . have you told anyone?" the woman named Suri asked.

"Told anyone what, Suri?"

"About Shiva. Have you told your family?"

Jeremy heard Dr. Miller put something down on his desk, and Jeremy imagined it was his reading glasses. Jeremy saw that Suri had her hands behind her back and was rocking slightly back and forth. She looked very anxious.

Dr. Miller spoke again. "This is not easy, Suri, and I know what Brighton said about confidentiality. But the truth is, it'll be everywhere soon. A secret like this doesn't stay secret for long. Sooner or later it's going to explode into our world, and I mean a long time before it ends. Secretary Brighton, understandably, wants to delay this as long as possible. But it's inevitable. If you really feel like you have to tell your family . . . heck, they probably won't believe you anyway."

"They'll like that you called it Shiva," Suri replied, smiling. Jeremy wondered if Suri was being sarcastic or not.

"Well, remember, Suri, that rules are just guidelines—there to make sure most people follow them. We have more important things to worry about right now than following the rules, so if it would make you work harder, then tell your parents. You still have to come to work on time." Dr. Miller laughed, and so did the woman named Suri.

With that strange conversation, Suri excused herself and rushed out of the room. Jeremy's phone buzzed rapidly, and he managed to read:

Anna: Jer, what's going on. Is he coming or not?

Jeremy was too confused to respond, but as Suri

hurried out, she ran straight into an unsuspecting Anna as she pretended to measure the walls' dimensions for the hundredth time.

Anna yelped and stumbled backward because Suri was moving so fast down the hallway. The papers Suri held in her hand scattered to the floor. One drifted several feet away, and when Anna went to retrieve it she managed to take one photo—her phone was already in her hand.

"Oh, dear. I'm so sorry. I've just been in such a hurry!" Suri exclaimed, quickly picking up the papers.

"Oh no, no, I'm sorry," Anna explained, putting her phone back in her pocket so she could to help the woman pick up the rest of the papers.

Anna only saw a lot of numbers and equations she didn't understand. She thought she was looking at the documents too long, and had a jolting fear Suri could see her motive somehow. She handed Suri the documents and looked up into her eyes, trying not to betray her real reason for being outside Dr. Miller's office.

But Suri noticed nothing, apologized again, and hurried away with her stack of strange mathematical symbols. Anna silently exhaled, feeling exhilarated at getting the photo. She held her phone tightly inside her pocket, as if squeezing the phone tight enough would keep the photos from getting deleted.

5

CAUGHT

Later that night, March 21, 2016
Johnson Space Center

Jeremy felt dazed as he climbed down the ladder from the ceiling. Anna was standing near him, asking him if he heard anything, but he said nothing. He didn't know what to make of it himself. He felt like he must be on the most ridiculous reality show ever created—like *The Truman Show* or something. Any second now, some old B-list celebrity would pop out of the door and yell, "Psych! We really got you, there!"

But that didn't happen. As they drove back, Anna tried to make out what the photo of the piece of paper meant, but it was just a bunch of numbers.

Once they were all assembled in Jeremy's room, Anna and Dustin madly tried to decipher the pages, but Jeremy just sat and stared at the wall, thinking.

A fourty-five kiloton bomb . . . That sounds like an atomic bomb. Atomic bomb . . . Why would NASA talk about using one of those? And what was that about Shiva? And what was all that about secrecy? He had said something about "Secretary Brighton . . . " Isn't that the Secretary of State? Is the United States going to war?

"Dude?" Dustin said.

Jeremy snapped out of his reverie.

"Yeah, sorry. What's up?"

"We were just saying that these photos don't really show us anything, but I'll look into these numbers and Google them a bit, and see if anyone else is working with them. That way, we might be able to find some info. You didn't hear anything else . . . maybe something someone said?" Dustin asked, but he was still engrossed in the photos.

"No, I didn't hear anything," Jeremy lied.

Dustin thanked Anna and Jeremy for an exciting

night, and said he would see them at school the next day.

"Goodnight, man," Jeremy said.

Once Dustin left, Jeremy turned to Anna. "Hey, I did hear something," he said, "but I don't know. It seems really weird." Jeremy went over exactly what he had heard to Anna, who listened intently.

"You think it could be war?" she asked.

"Maybe, but why NASA? And I don't know, but it doesn't seem like Dr. Miller would work for the military."

"You never know, maybe he's making a lot of money."

Jeremy couldn't stop thinking about one line Dr. Miller had said: ". . . definitely before it ends." *It . . .* he thought. *What was he referring to?* This made Jeremy uneasy.

"Maybe they are planning a war," Anna said, shaking her head. "It doesn't make sense."

Anna sat silently for a while, playing with her hair

and thinking. Finally she spoke flatly, offering, "Let's follow Dr. Miller."

"What, are you crazy?"

"He sounds a little unconventional. Didn't you say he told that other scientist to break confidentiality and tell her parents about this . . . whatever it is that they are keeping secret? Maybe if we confront him about it, he'll tell us what it is?"

Jeremy thought about that, but still replied anxiously, "I don't know . . . If he tells my dad, I'd be out of a job for sure. My dad might even kick me out of the house."

"Come on, you said yourself the worst thing that would happen is that we get grounded. I feel like that's still the case, or even less likely since we won't be trespassing anywhere. Plus, if you do get kicked out, you could come live with me!" Anna joked.

"I don't know if your dad would be okay with that . . . " Jeremy smiled and kissed Anna.

It is possible Dr. Miller would tell us what happened

without informing JSC, or more importantly, my dad?
Jeremy thought.

"Okay, let's do it," Jeremy agreed, and Anna's eyes sparkled with mischief.

• • •

Across the street of the JSC, they sat waiting for Dr. Miller to depart. Most of the other workers had left, but Dr. Miller's car still had not. They sat, both of them thinking that a "stakeout" was much more romantic in the movies than in real life. They switched the radio on and off repeatedly, and Anna braided her hair while Jeremy tried to flip coins into the cup holder.

Finally, by ten o'clock, the white puff of Dr. Miller's hair bounced along as he walked to his unassuming Hyundai. Jeremy and Anna looked on apprehensively, their hearts racing. Dr. Miller left the JSC and accelerated onto the Gulf Freeway north toward the city center. Jeremy and Anna made sure to follow far behind Dr. Miller.

Dr. Miller weaved in and out of traffic, and Jeremy kept up. Dr. Miller's Hyundai took the University of Houston exit, going under the freeway and then taking a right on Cullen Street.

"Should we stop him or something?" Anna asked. Neither of them had thought about how to confront Dr. Miller about his work.

"Maybe we should wait. I don't think this is where he lives, judging by the neighborhood.

The Greater Third Ward, where they were driving through, was the part of town Anna's dad would not allow her to go to—especially not at night.

They continued to follow Dr. Miller as he turned left and right, going deeper into the Third Ward. Suddenly, he put on his blinker and parked on the side of the road, in front of a particularly dreary bar called Soldier's. They drove past Dr. Miller so he wouldn't think he was being followed, and parked ahead of him so they could watch.

"What's he doing?" Anna asked, but Jeremy just shook his head.

Dr. Miller had parked next to a group of lasciviously dressed women. One of them walked to the passenger window and began speaking to Dr. Miller, but Jeremy couldn't make out what she was saying. *This is so awkward* . . . Jeremy thought. Suddenly, Dr. Miller got out of the car and began speaking to the prostitute directly. He looked like he had a big smile on his face, and she was laughing at what was probably some kind of joke he was telling.

Anna held her hand over her mouth in disgust.

Dr. Miller was walking around the prostitute now, pointing at something in the sky and waving his hands around. The woman looked embarrassed. Then he put his arms around her and walked into Soldier's.

"What should we do?" Anna asked Jeremy.

"Let's try to get in!" he replied excitedly.

Jeremy pushed through the saloon doors to enter the Old West bar. Luckily there was not a bouncer standing out front. There were the stuffed heads of deer, bison, buffalo, and bear on the walls with swords mounted below them. Lone Star State flags were everywhere, and people in cowboy hats sat in booths along the walls, drinking Budweiser or whiskey. At a booth in the far end of the bar, Jeremy saw Dr. Miller's puff of white hair.

"What can I get you?" the bartender asked, seeing them enter.

"Uh," Jeremy replied. He hadn't planned on ordering anything. But standing there with his mouth open might draw attention.

"Two soda waters with lime," Anna replied easily.

Jeremy looked over at his girlfriend, surprised both by Anna's quick order and her strange drink choice.

The barman looked both of them up and down, and Jeremy thought, *Thank God, I didn't shave for the past week. Hopefully I look old enough to be in the bar.*

"Y'all are twenty-one?" the barman asked as if on cue.

"I'm twenty-two, he's twenty-one," Anna lied confidently.

The barman looked them over once more and then shrugged, saying, "Right."

"Why soda waters?" Jeremy whispered as the bartender poured their drinks.

"So it *looks* like we're drinking," she explained, "so we fit in here and don't look out of place.

Smart, Jeremy thought.

They got their drinks and took a seat in the booth adjacent to Dr. Miller. After a minute or two, the woman with him left to go to the bathroom and Dr. Miller went to the bar. Jeremy watched as Dr. Miller drank three shots of colored liquor, grimacing with each, before purchasing another beer and sitting back down.

"Jesus," Anna whispered to Jeremy. "He's thirsty."

Jeremy and Anna whispered to each other, wondering how they should approach Dr. Miller, who had returned to speaking with the woman across from him. Dr. Miller and the woman were also whispering to each other, so Jeremy couldn't hear what was being said without obviously eavesdropping on them.

"Come on, let's just ask him," Anna whispered to Jeremy, but he sat still and waited, listening.

When the woman went to use the restroom again, Anna could no longer handle it, and slid into the booth across from Dr. Miller.

"What is happening at NASA? What are you using an atomic bomb for? What is going to be destroyed? Is NASA helping the U.S. go to war with someone?" she asked.

Dr. Miller furrowed his brow and shook himself, as if to shed the "drunk" from his being, and his eyes went from Anna to Jeremy, who reluctantly sidled into the booth next to Anna. Dr. Miller narrowed his eyes at Anna.

Dr. Miller didn't answer, just took another sip of his beer while looking at the couple.

"How old are you?" Dr. Miller asked Anna.

"Twenty-two," She replied fiercely. "Are you going to answer me?"

"Why would I tell you the truth after you just lied to me?" Dr. Miller answered, giggling and hiccupping at the same time.

Jeremy looked over at Dr. Miller and then at Anna, and asked, "What are the Russian scientists doing at the JSC? I looked up some of their names, and Dr. Ivanov, he's a nuclear physicist, right?"

Anna looked surprised at Jeremy, who hadn't told her this piece of information.

After what seemed like minutes, Dr. Miller spoke, tripping over his words. "You're one of the lighting workers at JSC. You work for Genser Contractors. I can have you fired, you know."

Dr. Miller said the last sentence so drunkenly it seemed like one long slurred word.

"This is bigger than me keeping my job," Jeremy retorted.

Dr. Miller looked through the neck of the beer bottle as though inspecting it for some science experiment. Then he looked up and said, "We are trying to figure out how to blast a comet to smithereens." The old scientist giggled.

"A comet?" Jeremy asked, "Why would we need to blast a comet?"

Dr. Miller looked cross-eyed at Jeremy and Anna, and fumbled for his beer again.

"See this?" Dr. Miller said, showing them the half-filled bottle of beer with his right hand. "This is the beautiful Earth. And this," Dr. Miller picked up the salt shaker with his other hand, "is a relatively small icy body undiscovered until recently."

Then, Dr. Miller swung the salt shaker's butt toward the neck of the beer bottle, connecting cleanly with the dark glass of the bottle. Jeremy and Anna threw up their hands to protect their faces, and Dr. Miller began to laugh as the glass shards landed on the ground.

"Hey!" the barman yelled, hearing the violent sound of shattering glass.

"Sorry!" Dr. Miller said innocently. "The bottle must have fallen out of my hand."

Suddenly, the woman with whom Dr. Miller had been sitting appeared from the bathroom, and looked confused as she found two teenagers sitting in her spot across from the scientist.

"Young tastes, Dr. Miller?" the woman asked contemptuously.

"What?" Anna asked.

At that moment a second figure appeared, and this one was a bouncer. He gave the prostitute a once-over and asked, "Weren't you not supposed to come in here anymore?"

The woman glared malevolently at the bouncer, swung her purse over her back, and stormed out of the bar. Then the bouncer glanced suspiciously at Jeremy and Anna, shrugged, and walked back to his original post.

"That doesn't seem fair," Anna remarked. "You were the one who broke the glass."

"Yeah, well," Dr. Miller said, his tone growing morose, "life isn't fair."

Jeremy contemplated what he'd heard, and didn't want to believe the scientist.

"How could this happen?" Anna asked, a little angrily.

"It's just a bit of bad luck really, but Shiva is orbiting the Sun and so are we. In fact, a lot of Kuiper Belt comets are undiscovered, and many are hurtling through space. This one just happens to be very large. And on a collision path with Earth."

Suddenly, it seemed as though the scientist had had enough of the bar, and grabbed his car keys from the table. In his drunken state, however, he misjudged where the keys were and grasped at nothing on the table. Jeremy and Anna looked at each other.

"Do you want a ride home, Dr. Miller?" Jeremy asked.

Dr. Miller furrowed his brow suspiciously at the keys, as if they had magically moved at the last second to prevent his hand from grasping them.

"I think that's probably a good idea," Dr. Miller mumbled, still looking at his keys.

Jeremy and Anna left their untouched drinks on the table and walked out of the bar, Dr. Miller in tow. Anna got in the backseat of the car, allowing Dr. Miller to sit in the front.

"Dr. Miller, can I ask you something?" Anna asked.

"Yes. What is it?"

"You really think the comet is on its way to hit Earth?"

"Shiva, Destroyer of Worlds, is coming," Dr. Miller answered sardonically.

"What if it's an elaborate joke? What if you're mistaken . . . " Anna's voice trailed away.

As Robert drifted off to sleep he thought about the two teenagers and wondered if he'd made a mistake by telling them about the end of the world. These thoughts were soon whisked away as he sunk into a pleasant dream.

6

DETENTION

March 22, 2016
Dr. Miller's home, Houston

D r. Miller woke up the next morning with the pounding headache he had known was coming. He was still in his clothes from the night before, and wearily he got up, showered, and went downstairs to make some coffee. As he listened to the coffee drip, he listened to NPR and learned that Chile was going through a populist revolution. The journalist said the revolution came as a surprise because the president had always been a popular candidate. It was a mystery why the people had revolted against the government.

But Dr. Miller knew it to be because they had found out about Shiva. After all, they were the only country aside from Russia and the United States that had access to the data at one point, and they had some pretty good telescopes, too. The telescope they'd used to get a physical image of Shiva, ALMA, was in the Chilean Andes. Perhaps the anarchy had already begun, though he thought they must be able to share this data with other nations using the internet. He wouldn't have put it past the U.S. government to shut off all communication with Chile to buy its own people a little more time without anarchy.

Who knows? All that mattered to Dr. Miller now was working on Suri's proposal to start one of the gaseous jets that could divert the course of the comet so it did not hit Earth in thirty months' time. And this required a lot of patience.

• • •

Sleeping through his alarm, Jeremy arrived at school fifteen minutes late while his Calculus teacher was in the middle of a lesson. As he sat down, he noticed that Anna was not in her seat. This was strange, as she was nearly always on time.

Ms. Konig rolled her eyes at Jeremy when he walked in but continued her lesson undisturbed. They were going over advanced trigonometry, something they had learned last year, but all the students had forgotten. Dustin raised his hand.

"Dustin?" Ms. Konig said, narrowing her eyes. Dustin normally understood the work, meaning his question was probably a joke, or pointless.

"Okay, I get why we need to know geometry. I could see that becoming useful to us at some point. But why in the world would anyone—ever—need to use Trig?"

Even though it wasn't that funny, the class laughed. Jeremy would usually have answered Dustin, telling him that Trigonometry was useful for all forms of engineering and physics. *It won't be useful after the comet destroys Earth,* thought Jeremy. He looked around at all the kids in his class. The

Nerds in the front row, eagerly writing down every one of Ms. Konig's marker strokes. The kids in the back goofing around—even in Calculus class there were the "Kids in the Back." *All of it is pointless now,* Jeremy thought.

English class, by contrast, seemed much more important. They were reading a book called *The Trial,* by a depressed German named Franz Kafka. Every single page seemed hard to read, and the main character, a guy named Mr. K, was on trial for committing a crime, but he didn't know what he did. The judges and police wouldn't tell him, and he ran around his idyllic German community trying to find out how to become a free man again. Everything he did, though, seemed to create more problems for himself, and he looked hopelessly at life.

It had been one of Jeremy's least favorite books in one of his least favorite classes, but now, as he sat in class listening to his classmate with the hipster glasses read to them, he found it oddly relaxing. And relatable. Mr. K seemed to think the world was against him and that life was pointless when faced with his trial. Jeremy found himself thinking, *Mr. K is probably around forty or something, but I'm only seventeen . . . By the time Shiva hits Earth I'll be twenty . . .*

Suddenly, thoughts started coming into Jeremy's mind incredibly fast. The end of the world, and Anna, and his parents, and the girl he dated before Anna, Sarah. He couldn't think, and his head started to hurt. He felt incredibly anxious and shook his head, as if he could shake these racing thoughts away. It was getting hard to breathe.

When that didn't work, he raised his hand, interrupting the girl reading in the front, and asked, "May I use the restroom?"

But he didn't wait for a reply, and instead, half-conscious, stumbled through the maze of desks, banging his knee on someone's desk and knocking over the coffee on it. He barely noticed his classmate's yelp of surprised anger.

He got out into the hallway and put his hands on his knees, breathing heavily. Slowly, the anxious feeling that surrounded his entire being melted away. *In and out, in and out,* he thought, breathing slowly.

Within minutes he began to feel better.

"Jeremy . . . are you alright?" the teacher, Mrs. Presley, asked, putting a hand on his shoulder.

Jeremy looked at Mrs. Presley. She was a small woman, with big glasses that made her resemble the Divination teacher from *Harry Potter.* However, she was not nearly as weird.

"Thanks, Mrs. Presley, I'm fine. I don't know what happened."

"I think you just had a mild panic attack, hon. You'll be okay. Kafka does that to people, but don't worry, your life won't be like Mr. K's." She rubbed Jeremy's back reassuringly and smiled.

"Thanks . . . I think I'll just go wash my face in the bathroom."

"Hurry back, dear," Mrs. Presley winked.

Jeremy walked to the bathroom slowly, his head feeling clearer by the minute. He had never had a panic attack before; he always felt like that was something that happened to weak people. Now, though, he had a newfound respect for people who dealt with this. He hadn't been able to function and it was hard to breathe. A few more seconds of those racing thoughts and he would have passed out!

When he got in the bathroom he put some water on his face. It felt good to clean himself up, and as he stepped out of the bathroom, his phone buzzed.

Anna: Hey . . . meet me outside Mr. C.'s?

Mr. C. was Anna's History teacher. Jeremy walked toward the History classroom.

He turned the corner past the trophy case and walked toward Anna, who was pacing up and down the hallway outside her class, looking like she had just finished crying. When she saw Jeremy she ran over and hugged him tightly.

He hugged her in return, and they could feel each other's heartbeats. Then they stepped out of the main building of the high school and walked down the steps to the football field. A new track had just been put in, and they strolled on the rubber material, bouncing lightly up and down.

"You know what I was thinking?" she asked.

"What?"

"School doesn't really matter anymore. And it's not just high school—this isn't senioritis. It's all of it. Why go to college? I won't even be able to *graduate*."

"Yeah."

"Yeah?! All you say is yeah?"

"What else is there to say, Anna?" Jeremy asked, but Anna didn't answer.

They walked silently for a bit until Jeremy spoke up. "Did you tell your parents?"

At this, Anna actually laughed out loud. "My parents? My parents wouldn't believe a word I said. They'd think I was crazy."

Jeremy agreed. He hadn't told his father. He could picture his response. "Son, there must be some mistake." His mother would say, "Sure, honey, but maybe you're wrong? Who knows?" In her mind, though, she would be certain that Jeremy was incorrect.

"And kids . . . I'll never have kids," Anna muttered to herself.

Jeremy looked down, again unsure of what to say.

"Dr. Miller said there were a lot of people trying to work on saving us. Even the Russians and the Americans are working together," Jeremy offered.

"Jeremy, he was completely drunk and had picked up a prostitute! To me, that means he thinks it's hopeless. He's still trying, yeah, but the happy endings only happen in movies like *Deep Impact*. You really think they can stop a forty kilometer wide boulder from hitting Earth? And don't say, 'Well, we landed a man on the Moon.'"

Jeremy laughed. It was exactly what he was going to say.

"Well, at least we have a few years, right?" Jeremy responded, trying to cheer Anna up.

"Yeah, two whole years . . . Come on," Anna said, suddenly getting up.

Plus five months, Jeremy thought. With that, she took Jeremy's hand and guided him back into the main building. She looked around with a sort of nervous excitement before walking quickly down the hall, stopping in front of a door that read, "Maintenance."

Anna looked up and down the hallway one more time before opening the door and pushing Jeremy inside, a wild and mischievous smile on her face.

"Hey, what are you up to?!" Jeremy whispered as loud as he could. Whispering seemed like the right thing to do at the time, even though he was sure no one could hear them.

"Shh," she said, and kissed Jeremy hard on the mouth.

This made Jeremy shut up, and he managed to smile. Jeremy quickly forgot about everything else besides the small maintenance closet, and kissed Anna back. They walk-kissed backward into the dark closet, knocking against a broom, a mop bucket, and Anna hit her heel on a large vacuum cleaner, at which point she yelped loudly.

Jeremy put his hand over her mouth, and she winced, laugh-crying, holding her foot and bouncing up and down.

"Are you alright?!" Jeremy whispered, giggling.

"I just—"

Suddenly, a flash of light burst into the janitor's closet, blinding Jeremy and Anna, who put their hands in front of their eyes

"What is going on here?!" a deep voice boomed.

Uh oh, thought Jeremy. Anna half-swore and half-giggled. "Nothing," Jeremy lied.

"Why are you in here?" the voice commanded again.

"Um, we were going to do a bit of cleaning before the world ends!" Anna burst out laughing. She stood behind Jeremy and held out a mop.

"Ah . . . comedians too."

Jeremy's heart sank. It was the über-conservative Vice Principal Jenkins, who apparently had heard

Anna's fit of giggling. Jeremy looked wildly around the closet, as if there were some escape.

Vice Principal Jenkins grabbed Jeremy by the arm, and commanded they come with him to his office. They had no choice.

They followed Mr. Jenkins, heads bent down like prisoners, into the office.

Karina, Anna's friend, was the office aide that period, and she sat in the front office with her head in her phone. When they walked by, she looked up and exclaimed, "What's up, girl!?"

Anna shook her head and grimaced, silently telling Karina she was in trouble.

Karina returned a look of utter curiosity mixed with more than a bit of humor, and Jeremy stuck out his hand to high-five Karina.

"You think getting in trouble is cool?!" Mr. Jenkins bellowed behind his desk.

Maybe he saw me high-five Karina, Jeremy thought.

Anna and Jeremy were seated in front of him. Mr.

Jenkins was a fat man, very tall, with jet black hair. He had a handlebar mustache and thin glasses which looked squeezed onto his melon-sized head.

"No, sir," they said together.

Mr. Jenkins lectured them for what seemed like forever, about being present in class and the importance of a decent education. He warned them against doing this again, and how they were basically terrible people. Jeremy and Anna nodded, "yes-sirred," and "sorry-sirred" anytime Mr. Jenkins stopped to breath. He finished by telling them the normal punishment for this type of "lascivious" behavior is suspension.

"Suspension!" they both exclaimed. This would not look good on their college applications, as many of them said that they would reconsider acceptance in the event of a suspension.

"Mr. Jenkins, please—" Anna began.

"Miss Chenko. This is no time to argue. Now, I know that you both are two bright students. I am going to make an exception. I will call your parents tonight and notify them, and you will have detention for two weeks. Consider this a probation period. If I hear that you two so much as skipped one more class . . . " Mr. Jenkins threatened, leaving his punishment up to their imagination.

Jeremy looked at Anna and back at Mr. Jenkins, visibly glad he would not be suspended. His father would be furious, but now a bit less. He would probably receive the exact same lecture at home as he did from Mr. Jenkins.

"Now, go straight back to class, both of you."

They thanked Mr. Jenkins for the minor punishment, and Jeremy walked toward AP Calculus.

"We can still kiss during school, right?" Jeremy asked, mockingly.

Anna answered by planting her lips on Jeremy's, and walked to drama class.

7

AN UNEXPECTED PHONE CALL

April 14, 2016
Johnson Space Center

It was getting warmer in Houston. It had been two months since "Discovery Day"—what Robert considered their start date for work. They had been working diligently and intensely, and the first complete rocket had been fully designed and was now in the middle of construction. A good portion of land had been taken over near Cape Canaveral to facilitate the production of IPMs, or interplanetary missiles. Suri and Robert called them Imps for short, due to their surprisingly small size. They had decided that their best use of resources was to make missiles that could poke holes in the outermost layer of the comet.

If they timed these impacts right, they would be able to release the gaseous pockets inside the comet's interior. These releases would be more powerful than blasting big bombs repeatedly at the surface, so they were designed more for accuracy and maneuverability than size. In fact, almost all of the volume of the Imps themselves were used for fuel to get the Imp from Earth to the comet.

Robert's office had finally moved to the much larger conference room which could accommodate the tens of people working together. Inside the office were physicists and engineers from every continent except Antarctica.

"Ve hav ze numbers, AE, and ze Imps are progressing nicely. Two of our models from Russia exited ze atmosphere without concern, and are on path now. Ze third, however, malfunctioned," Dr. Ivanov said.

"Why, Dr. Ivanov?" asked Dr. Petrov.

"Error report should come vithin a few hours."

"Let's go over it, you'll take the lead? You can work with Dr. Campero," Dr. Miller said.

"Okay."

At this point Suri spoke up. "Sir, there's the matter of the public. It's getting closer to a breaking point with the internet. The NSA, working with CNN and Fox, have done a good job preventing any coverage of our work, but with the internet it's more difficult to control the public. There are several prominent websites who are accusing NASA of either building nuclear weapons, starting a war, or sending a mission to Mars."

"I agree. I believe that for now, an ignorant populace will allow us to further our pursuit of building countermeasures while the country is still stable," Dr. Campero noted.

As the scientists continued working, Suri excused herself and walked to Daniel Atkins's office, the PR head of Project Mars. He had been doing a terrific job, but the press had now become so intrusive about the new project that they wanted concrete details before going public with it. Robert had refused to assign even one scientist to this decoy project because to him it was a useless waste of time. *But it would be much more difficult to work on saving the world when it was destroying itself. Why didn't he see that?* she asked herself.

So, helping him meant adding one more job to her ever-growing "things-to-do-before-the-world-ends" list. She walked into Daniel's office, which was always open. It had a big rainbow flag on the front of it.

"This is bad, Suri," Daniel groaned when she walked in. "Chile found out . . ."

"What do you mean?"

"The entire nation. You know, they had the raw data, and their government tried to stop it, but you know with the internet, there's only so much I can do. Things were simpler before the internet."

"You didn't work before the internet, Daniel."

"Right," he sighed, continuing to type on his laptop.

"Well, why hasn't the news spread outside of Chile yet?" Suri asked.

"I have absolutely no idea. I'm only the PR person for NASA, Suri, not the entire United States. But I expect that someone higher than me has shut off everything."

"What do you mean, everything?"

"I mean literally everything. All communication. All Chileans' Facebook accounts are offline."

"What?!"

"All Snapchat and all Twitter handles. Anything. I can't even call Chile."

"That's insane."

"It really is. I'm surprised the one-hundred-thousand Chileans living in the United States haven't revolted or something. They can still buy flights, but there are no flights returning to the United States from Chile."

"That won't last long," Suri reasoned.

"Tell me about it. I mean, I tried telling the NSA that, but the White House apparently wants absolutely nothing to get through to the American people."

"What else is new . . . " Suri mumbled.

Suri then gave Daniel an extremely brief design of a rocket that might make it to Mars, which Daniel thanked her for.

"In case you're wondering what the public is hearing about Chile," he said while handing her a newspaper, as Suri walked out back toward the conference room.

When she got back, everyone had left, except for Robert.

"What's happening—" Suri began, but she stopped, seeing that Robert was on the phone.

He finished speaking, and looked at her.

"That was a man who identified himself as Mr. S. He said he worked for SpaceX, the private space company from California. They know about Shiva. They know . . . somehow . . . "

"What? How?" Suri asked.

"It doesn't matter how," Robert replied wearily. "They want to help."

"Okay, but how?" Suri asked skeptically.

"Well, they say they've moved most of their labor force to the gigafactory in Nevada, but instead of building batteries they're going to build rockets. And they want to coordinate with us."

"Whoa," Suri crossed her arms, "but we are already building our own rockets."

"More rockets couldn't hurt," Robert said, looking over the most recent models of Shiva's movement through space.

"More rockets sounds messy," Suri countered.

"Maybe," Robert sighed, looking up, "but we could use all the help we could get, and we should be thankful they didn't tell the entire world what's happening."

Suri thought for a moment. "You said they put most of their labor force into rocket production. What about the rest of it?"

"The guy wouldn't say, but it was something that

they said we would definitely be interested in—some kind of rocket ship." Robert paused. "There's one problem, though."

"Uh oh," Suri answered.

"Since the government has been so tight on security, they won't give the SpaceX people access to our database or even abilities to transfer documents, so we have to go to their facility in California."

Suri groaned.

"They were going to call us a long time ago, but didn't have anything fully operational so they wanted to tell us when they did."

"They got all that done in two months—two facilities completely retrofitted?"

"I guess," Robert answered noncommittally.

"Do you think we can trust SpaceX?"

Robert thought for a moment before replying. "I think we should give them a chance, because we are going to need all the help we can get."

"Do we tell Chief Goldberg?" Suri asked.

"I don't know. He's been doing a lot of

communication with President Chaplin and Secretary Brighton. I don't want him to think this is a bad idea and shut it down. I think that it's best to have as many people working on this project as possible. If we fail, there's an incredibly small chance the private sector will be able to pick us up. So we should check out what they have to offer before telling Goldberg."

"I agree," Suri answered, and before she left she put a newspaper in front of Robert. "There's another problem. Have you seen this?"

Robert looked down, seeing the front page article, titled, "Chile Dissolves Amidst Social Unrest."

He *hmph*ed loudly, and thought for a moment before responding. "So someone leaked the information there, right?"

"That's right," Suri said, impressed that Robert guessed it so quickly. "When do you think it'll happen here?"

"I don't know, but I hope all the defenses around all of our new facilities will hold. Remember, we have guns here, and when anarchy takes over, it won't be just a few people lighting fires in the streets. It'll be big, like everything else in America."

Suri shuddered, and left Robert to continue his work.

Robert looked to his right in the conference room now defiled with papers. He sat at the head of the table. He wore the same shirt for the third consecutive day, and couldn't remember the last time he'd cooked for himself, which was something he used to enjoy. He looked to the huge whiteboard on the right wall. It was filled with a long list of things to do. It had things like "Find a crew for possible manned mission" and "Design a manned mission" on it.

Right now, only the tasks in the upper left-hand corner of the wall were checked. Up next were small tasks, since Project Mars was still very much in the preliminary stages. There was plenty to do to support the building of rockets and gathering nuclear weapons until Shiva came closer to Earth. Still, Robert was impressed by what they had done so far.

They had identified the orbital path of Shiva very

closely. Without any outside influence, its orbit path would hit Earth in approximately thirty months. Using the gaseous explosions and jets of unfrozen hydrogen, methane, and ammonia gas released by the Imps, he hoped to move the comet out of the collision path. The comet's approach would be utterly terrifying, but it would look incredibly beautiful as it loomed large in the sky. Robert would make a mental note that—when anarchy commenced—he would walk right into Best Buy and steal the best camera and lens combination he could find and use it to take some photographs of the comet. The comet would have a glowing "outgas," or tail of gas, and a second "dust tail," which would trail the comet for thousands of miles, making it possibly the most beautiful night sky ever seen by humans. Of course, the dinosaurs had likely seen something just as beautiful before it vaporized them into dust.

When the comet got closer to the Sun, its solar rays would act like a microwave and cook the comet from the outside in. Due to the comet's elongated elliptical orbit and its spin, the Sun would heat its sides unevenly. Because of this, the comet's heat wouldn't distribute evenly across its surface, and some parts of the comet would get hotter than others, much like when you cook an oddly formed potato in the microwave. At some point this would create a chink in the comet's frozen armor. Then, the gas below this chink would explode out, hopefully acting like a little jet engine, which was actually how comets got those beautiful tails. The Imps would target these engines on one side of the comet in order to maximize this thrust. The problem was that, obviously, something like this had never been tried before. And bombing the comet could have unintended consequences, like it breaking, or the gaseous jets releasing in the wrong direction. The good thing was that the mathematical modeling that could be done with the supercomputers today were very accurate, very efficient, and took into consideration much of the uncertainty that stoked Robert's unease. Most of the work now just consisted of writing a ton of code, and then sitting back.

All of this work gave Robert—along with Suri and just about everyone else at NASA—very tired fingers and very sore eyes.

As Robert finished up his last piece of code for the night, he went over recent numbers for satellite production. Suddenly, his phone rang. *Odd,* he thought. He didn't recognize the number.

"Yes?"

"Dr. Miller?" A nervous voice replied over the phone.

"Who's this?"

"This is uh . . . Jeremy Genser. Um, my girl-friend and I met you a few weeks ago when we, well, followed—"

"Yes, Jeremy, I remember you, and Anna as well. How can I help you?" Robert didn't remember giving the kids his phone number. He felt a little ashamed for telling them the world was going to end, and wanted to make sure they were okay.

"Well, we, um, took something and now we are feeling not so good."

Great, Robert thought, *this is totally not on my to-do list.* He could hear Anna screaming in the background, "It's all going to end!!"

"We probably shouldn't drive."

"Yes, Jeremy. Smart of you to acknowledge. Where are you?"

Jeremy texted Robert the address, and he looked one more time at his list. He finally thought that they were getting a handle on things. It seemed, though, that telling Jeremy and Anna about the end of the world may not have been the best idea. *Oh well, live and learn*, he thought.

Robert drove through the streets of Houston to Spotts Park, a patch of green around the Buffalo Bayou, which meandered slowly through the Houston metropolis. A few days of heavy rain had made the little river overflow, and its banks were thick and muddy. Robert found Anna and Jeremy sitting on a bench, which only barely jutted out of the water. Their bare feet were in the mud, kicking it around.

Robert grimaced, but he remembered what it was like to be young. He couldn't imagine what they must be going through. At least he had lived almost an entire life. They had only just started theirs.

"Hi, Dr. Miller," Anna said, dreamily.

Robert walked over, sighing at the fact he would need to buy new shoes, as his were immediately caked with mud.

"Do you really think you can save the world?" Jeremy asked.

Robert thought about it while looking at Houston's reflection in the muddy water.

"I really don't know, but what I can tell you is that humanity has been able to overcome some pretty substantial odds to survive in its history. So I think that even though it might be scary to fight against this seemingly impossible task, we have to try."

"It's crazy to think that all of this civilization that we've built—the huge skyscrapers, the literature, all of it—could just be gone, just because a random piece of rock got in the way of Earth . . . " Jeremy said.

Robert put his arm around Jeremy. "It won't all be gone. We'll find out a way. But soon, our country is going to disintegrate. The government is going to take over everything—the communication, all of it. I don't know when, but the world will go up in flames. Maybe it would be good to be away from it all, unless you find a way to help."

8

PRESIDENT CHAPLIN

April 15, 2016
Johnson Space Center

Robert sat in the large conference room again, typing away at his computer. To his left sat Dr. Goldberg, straightening his tie. Daniel Atkins sat to Dr. Goldberg's left, typing as well. Any minute now they would have a video conference with Secretary Brighton, President Chaplin, and her Chief of Staff and Press Secretary.

Robert saw Dr. Goldberg wringing his hands, and then wiping them off of his pants.

"Relax, Goldberg, it'll be okay. It's only the president. One might say—"

"No offense, Miller, but I don't need your pep talk right now. Thanks."

Robert shrugged and President Chaplin appeared on the largest of the monitors, and the other faces appeared on smaller screens below her. Everyone stood up, and Robert watched Chaplin. He didn't vote for her, but that was only because he didn't vote. She was an imposing woman; you could see it in her eyes. They were a deep radiant blue, fierce with passion, and it felt as though this was where she got her power. Her smile, though, which she exhibited shortly after she came on the screen, was her charm. You felt warm and comfortable and safe when Chaplin looked at you.

"Good morning, lady and gentlemen," Chaplin said warmly, nodding for everyone to sit down, which they did.

"Good morning, Madam President," everyone said in unison.

The air was thick in the conference room.

"I called this meeting," President Chaplin began,

"for two reasons. Firstly, to meet Dr. Miller and his team. I understand you are working around the clock to ensure Earth's safety, and for that I want to thank you. Also—please, Doctor, call me Victoria. You are saving the world here. I'm just here to make sure you have what you need."

The other Cabinet members were visibly bothered by President Chaplin's informal gesture. Dr. Miller felt honored, and Suri beamed at her president.

President Chaplin continued, "The second reason I called this meeting is to get everyone on the same page. This is now a global crisis. Chile, as you know, has descended into anarchy. Its scientists released photographs of Comet J312 to the public, which we believe is the reason for the government's fall. As we begin to fire massive amounts of explosives out of the atmosphere, this is bound to cause domestic uproar for us as well. There are many things we must account for.

"Peru and Bolivia have both fallen as well, and it's only a matter of time before the rest of South

America descends into anarchy. As a result, I have shut down communication between the citizens of these three nations and our own citizens. Predictably, this has caused some . . . complaints . . . among our own population. We have even shut off all flights and trade between Santiago and the United States. The secret of the meteor won't last forever."

"Comet," Robert interrupted. "It's a *comet*, not a meteor."

"Right, *comet*, whatever. As I was saying, over the past two months, the U.S. has taken over complete control of the major news networks, and we have been in touch with Facebook and other social media sites. They have agreed to keep America at peace for a little while longer.

"We will do everything we can to make sure the United States of America, and the world, keeps going to work, keeps paying their bills, and keeps on living. This is essential to us continuing to live and prosper, and most importantly, stop *Comet* J312 from hitting our planet." The president paused, and then continued. "Ideally, we will do this as discreetly as possible."

Robert and Suri looked at each other.

"Next week I will announce Project Mars to the public, a plan to put a team of astronauts on the Red Planet within two and a half years. Obviously, secretly we will be working—"

At this Robert spoke up. "President Chaplin, if I may, you can't seriously expect to keep the American people in the dark about Shi—about Comet J312?"

President Chaplin exhaled, and in answer the screen faded to black and was replaced by a video of a burning church in the middle of a big square.

President Chaplin's voice came over the video. "The footage you're seeing now is from one week ago. The Chilean news station 'Canal 24 Horas' published the news of the comet, and after a calm night, the streets erupted into chaos and anarchy. Churches and government buildings around the capital were burned, and generals took up arms against the government. The country has been in a relative state of anarchy ever since." The scenes on the screen switched now to different cities, where fighting was similarly taking place as President Chaplin's voice continued. "Here is La Paz, Bolivia, and Lima, Peru. This is what happens when the people discover the world is going to end."

President Chaplin's head returned on the screen, wearing a sad, despondent face, and she spoke up again toward the now-silent scientists. "I know it may seem like the wrong thing to do, but the longer we can work as a stable country, the better chance we have of saving the world.

"Already, the activist groups Anonymous and WikiLeaks are trying to hack and discover what is happening and publish it to the world. So far, we believe we have them convinced that Project Mars is what they want to uncover, and not the comet itself.

"The people of the United States believe in us, but when faced with the destruction of the planet, well, I'm not sure I want to risk it just yet. Remember, our primary objective is to save the world. When things get bad here, remember that. We do not worry about loss of freedom, we do not worry even about security. We serve the USA and the world, and in this, we must make sure the Earth survives. After all"—the president gave a wry smile to the camera—"the Earth is a pretty nice spot in the solar system, isn't it?"

The scientists looked at each other and nodded, and then Victoria Chaplin continued, "I'm telling you all this because for one, I want you to respect—and agree with—the idea that we should keep this quiet as long as possible. Secondly, I would like you to delegate a team of scientists to working on a 'leave Earth' option—a preliminary estimation on how long we can stay in a self-sustaining vessel, perhaps to orbit the Earth during and after the impact event. This is in case the collision course is unavoidable. We must explore our alternatives."

Robert began to speak, but held his tongue. *An alternative to Earth?!* he thought.

"Do you have any questions for me?" Chaplin asked.

No one seemed to have anything of note, and there was a small moment of silence. Suri and Robert breathed deeply. They both felt that even if every scientist and person "in the know" held their tongue, this secret was too big to keep.

"Very well. I will come back in one week's time to hear an update on how things are going. Good luck. We have the best minds in the world on this project, and the fate of the world is in your hands. God bless the United States of America."

We'll need a lot more than God's blessing, Robert thought.

9

JEREMY'S PLAN

May 3, 2016
Sam Houston High School

"You're quitting the basketball team?!" gasped Jasper, Jeremy's basketball team captain. "Are you kidding me? Now?!" They stood in the hallway during school. Kids scurried around them walking and talking a mile a minute.

Jeremy hadn't exactly meant to quit. They were already in the playoffs, and their coach had given them a whole new set of plays to learn for practice next week. Normally, Jeremy would have excitedly tackled the task—he loved learning new tactics for his favorite sport—but nothing seemed normal anymore, and basketball was not on his mind.

"Why are you quitting?" Jasper asked.

Suddenly, an underclassmen ran into them while looking down at his phone, looked fearfully up at the two seniors, and hustled out of sight.

Oh, I don't know . . . the world is going to end maybe, Jeremy thought. But he couldn't come up with a real answer. He couldn't even lie and say his dad wouldn't let him play. His father was one of the team's biggest fans.

"If you can't come up with a real answer—like the world is about to end—I'm not letting you quit."

Jeremy burst out laughing and doubled over. Jasper seemed pleased his joke landed so well, even if he didn't really think it was that funny. Jeremy finished laughing and looked up at Jasper, taking the plays from his hand.

"Alright, man. I'm sorry, I'm just stressed I guess. Girl problems. I'll study them for next week's practice."

Jasper narrowed his eyes at Jeremy. "Alright,

bud. Don't worry so much, man. It's high school. Supposed to be fun, ya' know?"

"Thanks, Jasper."

"Oh! Wait, man, I forgot to ask you something."

"What's up?" Jeremy asked.

"This weekend a few of us are heading to my beach house in Galveston. Want to come?"

"Galveston?" Jeremy asked, but his mind was somewhere else.

"Yeah, man, you've been there. My parents aren't gonna be there this weekend, so I figured we could go."

"Um, I can't, but thanks a lot! I appreciate it!"

Of course! Jeremy thought.

Jasper had unwittingly given Jeremy a great idea, and Jeremy weaved in and out of his classmates, arriving at English class. He was one of the first people there. He quickly sat down, got out a pencil and a scrap of paper, and began to write. Mrs. Presley was grading at her desk and looked up to see Jeremy seated, quickly scribbling, apparently impressed, but

Jeremy wasn't writing anything school-related. It was probably the first time in his life he wasn't writing something for school.

Jeremy wrote, *Things I'll need for the End of the World.*

He excitedly worked through his list, creating subcategories for places he would need to go. *Home Depot* would have things under it like *hammer*, *nails*, and *a nice ax*, with prices listed next to them. In big letters he wrote *GAS!* And right under that, *gas canisters.* By the end of the class he had filled up, front and back, an entire list of things he thought he'd need.

His plan was not very elaborate, but it gave him some hope. During lunch he found Anna, and showed it to her.

"What is this?" she asked.

Jeremy got straight to the point.

"I think we should drive to your cabin, in Vail."

"Now? You want to drive all the way to Colorado, now?"

"We should leave before the U.S. dissolves,"

Jeremy spoke in a hushed tone, explaining himself, "You heard what was happening around the world, and what Dr. Miller said. What's the point of going to school now, anyway? Who cares? Let's just go to your cabin and live. And more importantly, hide from the anarchy that's going to come. I bet things will get crazy here when people hear about Shiva."

Jeremy wanted nothing more than to simply live with Anna, without responsibility, without sacrificing precious days that could be spent hiking, swimming, relaxing, and hanging out with his friends. Spend your last days on Earth in a classroom—yeah right!

"I don't know, Jer. What about our parents? I'd want them to come with us."

"Ask them. I'm going to ask mine, too. And I'm going to ask Dustin to go, too. Since he lives with his aunt and they don't get along, I think he'll come. Basically, we could live together, you know. How about that?"

Anna looked up at him, surprised. "Really?"

"Of course!"

"Oh, Jeremy!" Anna said, embracing Jeremy tightly, and kissing him lovingly. She stroked his hair and said goodbye. Jeremy could swear she skipped to class on the way back.

Jeremy cut class, got into his car, and drove straight to the bank. He went to the ATM and plugged in his pin to check how much money he had in his account—$952.41. He went into the bank since he couldn't withdraw it all at once from an ATM, and asked the teller if he could get large bills.

"Are you sure you want to deplete your account?" she asked, curiously.

"Leave fifty dollars. Yes, thank you."

The bills made his wallet thick and he felt anxious about the possibility of getting robbed. He drove to Home Depot and walked in, nodding to the teller, and asked for the "nails" aisle. He walked up and shook his head when he saw the vast wall of nails of all lengths, widths, types of heads, even all types of colors! It was maddening.

I'll just take nails out of buildings if I need them I guess, he thought.

If he bought a bunch of nails and stuff, he would need a box, and Jeremy realized he didn't plan everything nearly enough. Instead of buying everything, he decided to raid his father's garage and truck for equipment before leaving. This also meant he had money to buy a generator, which he knew they would need. This way, they would be able to charge anything they needed, like phones, GPS, whatever. The generator was $400.00, and money well spent.

After that, Jeremy drove to Dustin's house.

His car was out front because he had a free seventh period. His aunt, Andrea, answered the door.

"What do you want?" the woman asked.

"Hi, Mrs. Wood. Is Dustin there?"

"Aren't you supposed to be in school right now?"

Jeremy gulped and then lied, "No, we have a half day today. It's a teacher work day."

"Oh, good for you. Yes, he's here, working on some kind of *art project*." Andrea said the last words hatefully, but moved slightly, allowing Jeremy to go inside.

"Oh, right. Thanks, Mrs. Wood."

He walked up the spiral staircase to Dustin's room, gazing at the chandelier that he walked around, before knocking at his door.

"Come in."

"What's up, man?"

"Oh, hey, Jeremy! What do you think?" Dustin looked behind him, and showed Jeremy a large canvass. Jeremy burst out laughing. It was an incredibly detailed painting of Dustin's own naked body.

"I'm going to give it to Karina."

"You're so weird, man."

"I think she'll like it," Dustin mused.

"I think she will either punch you in the face or run away screaming."

"Maybe both!"

Dustin offered Jeremy a Gatorade and opened his window, which led to the roof. They climbed outside and sat, overlooking the Houston skyline. The rain had lessened over the past week, but they still spotted a little flooding. It was a mark of Houston, the spring floods, and Jeremy looked at his city fondly in the shimmering midday heat.

"So, what's up? You're supposed to be in Physics class, right?"

"Yeah, I skipped it. I wanted to tell you something . . . "

Then Jeremy told Dustin what he hadn't told Dustin the day they went to the JSC and spied on Dr. Miller. He told Dustin about following Dr. Miller down to the Third Ward and the bar Soldier's, and then when he came to see them at the Buffalo Bayou. He told him everything, including his most recent plan of heading to a remote area of Vail, high in the Rocky Mountains—Anna's parent's cabin.

"I can't believe it," Dustin answered. "That's what those numbers and stuff were? The stuff that Anna saw? That's so terrible."

Though Dustin believed Jeremy, it didn't really

sink in yet, but nevertheless he looked over at his oldest friend and said, "I'm in."

Dustin hadn't reacted the way Jeremy thought he would—by throwing the Gatorade bottle off the roof, or shouting at the top of his lungs. He just looked down, like he suddenly got exhausted when the words entered his ears. But, as always, Dustin was at his side. That's why Dustin was Jeremy's best friend—he stood beside him no matter what.

"Are you going to tell your parents?" Dustin asked.

"Yeah, but I keep putting it off. Anna's going to tell her parents, but they won't believe her. Are you going to tell your aunt?'

"She wouldn't leave Houston if aliens landed on the bayou."

They sat quietly for a while.

"You know," Dustin said, thinking, "this actually explains something."

"What does?"

"You remember Francisco, the Chilean exchange

student we had? I tried asking him about the revolution and the fighting going on in Santiago right now, but I couldn't reach him on Facebook. It was like he deleted his profile, which I thought, okay, people delete their Facebook, but then I sent him a WhatsApp message, and that didn't get to him either. Then email, and it also wouldn't work. It was like he had vanished from the internet.

"But maybe . . . " Dustin's voice grew suspicious. " . . . Maybe someone is blocking internet traffic between our countries?"

"You know the president's speech about Project Mars?" Jeremy said, ignoring Dustin's question. "It's just a cover for the real plan."

Dustin smirked. "For knocking the meteor out of our way?"

"Actually, it's a comet."

"Whatever."

They sat in silence for a while, drinking Gatorade and watching two birds circle over a swimming pool a few houses down. Then Dustin spoke up.

"We should get supplies. And when do you want to leave?"

. . .

Daniel Atkins sat in an ornate office in the White House. The White House Press Secretary, Justine Richards, typed away on her desktop computer. She was a rather large woman with a shrill voice. She was incredibly crass in person, but when it came to delivering politically correct and bipartisan statements, she was the best there was. Together, they were in charge of Shiva's cover-up and the Project Mars charade, and things were not going all that smoothly.

Anonymous, the hacking group responsible for much of the WikiLeaks data dumps and many other cyber-crimes, had hacked NASA's servers. Daniel guessed they were after more concrete details regarding the budget, or perhaps blueprints of the ship being designed to reach Mars. Instead, they stumbled upon the datasheets of one of the Interplanetary Missiles.

Anonymous had then contacted Justine, asking for more information, and threatened to go to the press. However, when Justine ignored this (all the major news networks were now government controlled), Anonymous went to CNN. CNN, however, did not publicize the data. So, Anonymous had called back, threatening to send it to WikiLeaks, which, after Justine ignored them a second time, they did.

Anonymous asked Justine about aliens: Is that why they were building rockets that could leave Earth with nuclear weapons?

Still, Justine and Daniel had decided that making something up about the weapons was unwise (what could they say, that the U.S. was planning to blow up satellites with nuclear weapons? In the name of national security?), so again they had decided to say nothing. The NSA shut down and enacted what they called "Cyber–Martial Law," which, in conjunction with Facebook, Twitter, and other social media sites, severely restricted the information that could be seen by Americans on the internet.

So Anonymous called back a third time, threatening that they would doctor evidence about an alien invasion if the NSA didn't come clean on what the missiles would be used for, to which the NSA predictably replied with silence.

Then, a previously unknown, unaffiliated hacker had exposed the United States as the people who had mysteriously shut down communications between the U.S. and three South American nations: Chile, Peru, and Bolivia. This unaffiliated hacker went by the handle "@OneUnionAnarchist."

A great deal of distrust was stirring among the people. Daniel felt that honest and sincere communication was the best possible method. He felt that it was paramount that they get the initial anarchy out of the way, and just tell the American people the truth. It would be ideal if they could stop the comet hitting Earth without telling the public like the president wanted, but this was looking increasingly unlikely.

The internet was simply too vast to secure. Daniel fidgeted with his fingers while his laptop started up. Justine began to speak without turning her attention away from her computer.

"So, the most likely scenario for how the public will begin to know what is happening is through a leak or a hack, and the internet will spread out the information to the population," Justine began. "Frankly, I'm surprised Americans—especially those with family in Chile—are not more angry about us shutting down their communication with their families. Then again, we are also silencing their protests in the West and other large cities . . . " Justine seemed to be talking to herself about what to do.

"Justine," Daniel interrupted, "what about when it does go public? We need more of a plan than we have right now. We can't just tell them we are going to shoot a bunch of small rockets at the comet; we need a plan to make sure the people don't lose faith. Maybe we should be honest with the people?"

"Yes, but no matter what we tell them, the people

will be incredibly scared. Like the president said, we will focus on delaying the truth for as long as possible."

"What if telling the people makes them motivated to work?" Daniel replied. "Motivated to help in the cause?"

"It's not worth it," Justine replied flatly. "Too risky."

"You know," Daniel accused angrily, "since when did you become Minister of Propaganda? I thought this was the land of the free?"

"Not when a comet is about to destroy the entire world. Few things are more important than freedom, but survival is one of them."

"This is a mistake," Daniel growled, to his own surprise. He then stormed out of the office, and drove to the airport to get back to Houston.

10

CYBER HACK

June 11, 2016
Dustin's house, Houston, Texas

Dustin showed Jeremy the computer screen at his house. Anna and Karina were there too, looking over at the curious file that had gone viral. "This is it," he said. "This is when the world we know is ending . . . "

Jeremy squinted his eyes at the information. It was a document circulating through social media, which was a file from someone called "@ OneUnionAnarchist," and seemed to show some information about Shiva, but it was difficult to decipher what it was. There were certain parts of the document that were highlighted in bright yellow on the screen. It spoke about "Comet J312 arrival date approximately June 14th, 2018" as well as "40km diameter," and "Extinction-level Event."

"We should leave as fast as we can," Jeremy said, "I think people will start to lose their minds, don't you? I don't know what's going to happen but it can't be good."

Jeremy was nervous. He had read in history books about WWII, and how a lot of the people that stayed behind thinking everyone would be okay ended up caught in the middle of a world war, but Dustin and Anna were more reluctant to leave. They convinced Jeremy to wait at least until the end of the week to see what would happen. Jeremy reluctantly agreed, but packed everything up for the trip just in case.

One week after the news had leaked, Jeremy breathed a sigh of relief. In fact, most of those who read the leaked document were already conspiracy theorists, so most people shrugged the news off like anything else. And since Fox News, CNN, and *The New York Times* all agreed with each other, people relied on major news networks like they always had. *You'd be surprised what people refuse to believe, even if it's right in front of their face,* Jeremy thought.

There were some outliers, though. Little reports on fringe news sites of "anarchist" communes being set up, and even an "ark" being built for the über-wealthy. Unfortunately, these were also websites that said aliens were real, so for many it was hard to tell fact from fiction. Jeremy watched the news as the wars in Syria and the fighting in Afghanistan had stopped, and there were celebrations of all the troops coming home.

There were huge parades for the military's return home—one even in Houston—but Jeremy thought it was odd when he didn't see smiles on the returning soldiers' faces. They should have been happy, but instead their faces looked as grim as when they left for war.

By the eighth day after the @OneUnionAnarchist document, a few religious groups had begun preaching about the coming apocalypse, and projected its end date. When Karina had come over to Anna's house that night, Anna had planned on telling her the plan to go to Vail before the news became any more public, because for now everyone acted more or less the same. Karina beat her to it, though, when she stepped into Anna's room.

"The priest at my church today said that the world is going to end, and I don't believe him, but he is a smart guy. It is weird to see him so sure of something so crazy . . . " Karina shook her head, confused.

"Yeah . . . about that," Anna said, and confirmed for her the priest's thoughts.

After the initial denial came distraught weeping. Anna then told Karina about the plan to head to Vail. She agreed to go, but wanted to bring Milo, her German Sheppard.

"You're not worried about your parents?" Anna asked.

"I don't get along with my parents," Karina said flatly.

After Karina left Anna's house, Anna called Jeremy

to tell him that Karina was on board for Vail. They agreed to leave in five days, in Dustin's car.

. . .

Suri and Robert had organized their final push into the three distinct projects that President Chaplin had asked for. They researched deeper into a "gravitational pull" plan, which, as it turned out, would be useful when Shiva came closer to Earth. It consisted of firing a large amount of heavy material to one side of the comet, which would exert a gravitational force on it, making it move. It would change its kinetic energy only slightly, but if "almost nothing" is the difference between extinction and life, it could definitely come in handy.

The second plan was also their current strategy, which consisted of sending nuclear missiles to poke holes in the comet's solid exterior to produce the propulsive jets to push it away from Earth.

The last plan to leave Earth was, according to

Robert, "beyond stupid," and he planned to tell the president this. It was impossible for human life to exist without Earth for any meaningful amount of time, and Robert felt that they should focus on saving the almost seven billion people on the planet instead of "letting a chosen few ride around in a spaceship" as Robert put it. He refused to speak about it.

As always, this meant more work for Suri. Unfortunately, when they arrived at the normal conference room to meet with the president, they found Secretary Brighton sitting there instead. Robert groaned.

Suri and Robert explained the three different plans of attack and the Secretary said he would brief the president. To Suri's credit, Robert did note that her design for the ark was quite intelligent, and that if it didn't require so many resources to build, he would actually want to work on it. Maybe, if they did manage to save the world, it would be a fun future side project.

They were about to leave the conference room

when Secretary Brighton cleared his throat. "I'm sure you heard that someone has leaked the information about the meteor to the press—"

"—Comet," Suri mumbled.

"Huh?" Secretary Brighton blinked at Suri, then resumed his speech. "Now, Fox, CNN, NBC, and the other news networks haven't published the information yet, and we tried to shut off all the direct sources as fast as we could, but it wasn't enough. San Francisco and Seattle are both experiencing areas of civil unrest, and from phone taps and computer taps we know that most people in these cities believe that a meteor will destroy the Earth."

"Comet," Suri mumbled, "*again*."

"Whatever! Anyway, there have been numerous break-ins, people are buying guns, emptying their bank accounts, and stockpiling food. It's only a matter of time before the rest of the country does too, so we decided we'll have a press release in six days. We'd like you two to be there to answer any questions the media has about the *comet*, and do us a favor. Tell them that it's not that big of a deal—that you are going to save the world without a doubt. That will give us all a lot of much needed peace and security."

Suri spoke first, "But sir, we have no idea right now, and to be honest it's not looking too good—"

The Secretary overrode her voice. "It's not about that now. We must make sure that our people do not descend into chaos like the rest of the world is starting to. We have little choice at this point; our world is depending on you and your team to find a solution to this problem. We have to give them faith."

Robert had found his mind wandering during this speech, and after leaving work, he went to where it had wandered off to. He walked along the familiar sidewalk on Forty-second Street, his hands in his pockets. He saw the Victorian houses, nestled neatly alongside each other. He walked past the white picket fence, and turned right at small house with the red painted door.

Robert walked along the path to the front porch,

and hesitated before knocking on the door. All of a sudden, in the window to the right of the front door, two eyes appeared. They startled him, and he could hear a small child's voice from inside the house.

"Daddy! Someone's here at the door!" the little girl yelled, still looking at Robert.

When the door opened, a man in his thirties greeted Robert with a warm smile, and the child hugged the man's legs, a little scared. The kid gazed up at Robert, who looked down at the small child, and found himself trying his hardest not to cry.

"Can I help you?" The man asked, cheerfully.

Robert lost courage when he saw the child. "Um, yes. I'm sorry, I think I have the wrong hou—"

Suddenly, a voice from behind Robert spoke up as he turned to leave.

"Hey honey, I think this is for me."

"Jennifer," Robert gasped, seeing his estranged daughter again. She looked breathtaking, if it wasn't for the scowl across her face. She had his eyes, and from her countenance, he guessed his stubborn personality.

"Hi, Dad."

At this point, the man shifted uncomfortably at the front door, and told the little girl to go inside.

"So, it's you," the man said, turning to Robert and closing the door, his child still inside the house, now peering out of the window again.

"Listen, it's nice to meet you, uh—" Robert began.

"Frank," the man said, steely-eyed.

"Right, well. I just need a quick word with my daughter and then you can say or do whatever you want. It looks like you want to punch me in the face, so you can even do that."

"Dad, what is it you want? Whatever you can say to me you can say to Frank. I'm glad you two are finally meeting, by the way," Jennifer said, sarcastically.

Robert sighed deeply, wishing his daughter was a little less stubborn than himself.

"The world is going to end, Jennifer."

Jennifer rolled her eyes.

"Yeah, I know, Dad. Nothing is permanent, and we are all just atoms in this great big—"

"June 15th, 2018, give or take a few days, a comet of around forty kilometers in diameter will come into contact with Earth, and most likely kill everyone on this planet."

Jennifer, always the skeptic, asked, "Most likely?"

"Unless I stop it."

" . . . Dad?"

Jennifer tried to find any trace of deception in her father's eyes, but only found a mix of sadness and determination. Then Jennifer asked, "When did you find out?"

"Around the middle of February."

Jennifer punched her father in the chest.

"And you waited until now to tell me?"

Jennifer looked irate until Robert spoke again. "I'm sorry, Jennifer. I wanted to come sooner, but, well, I wanted to be sure, and I also haven't had much time to get away." He sighed. "Jennifer, I think you and your family need to get out of the city."

"You mean leave?" Jennifer asked, dumbfounded. "Leave where? You just told me a comet is going to destroy Earth. I'm not moving to Mars."

At this, Robert started tearing up, but tried to keep his voice stable. "I'm not asking you to move to Mars. This isn't about me, Jenn, I'm trying to protect you. President Chaplin is going to publicly announce the comet's arrival in one week, and it wouldn't surprise me if the country dissolves into chaos. Who will follow laws when the world will end, right?"

Robert noticed that Frank was looking blankly from Robert to Jennifer.

"Jenny, you don't really believe this man, do you?"

"Frank, my father hasn't spoken to me in ten years, and we haven't seen each other a long time before that, but he is a brilliant astrophysicist working for NASA. He wouldn't break this silence for anything. He's telling the truth." She took a look back at her daughter before continuing. "You think we should go somewhere less populated, right? A place where the crazy anarchists won't hurt us."

"Exactly."

They were quiet for a while, and Frank excused himself to take care of their daughter, leaving Jennifer and Robert alone. They sat on the front porch next to each other, and finally, for the first time since Robert heard about the comet, he began to cry. Slowly at first, but slowly the small tears turned into weeping sobs, and Jennifer put her head on his shoulder and rubbed his back.

They sat together for half an hour, watching the cars go by Jennifer's house.

"You know, my friend Danielle called me yesterday, saying that she heard something about the world ending, but I told her not to worry, not to believe everything she reads," Jennifer laughed. "She called me two months ago to tell me about some 9/11 conspiracy theory they released, too, and I brushed it off. Maybe that one was right, too."

Robert laughed warily.

"You really think it will get crazy?" Jennifer asked.

"Chile has already overthrown its government. We aren't all that different from one another—Chilean, American, Ghanaian, whatever. We are all people, all scared of death, all trying to live some way we think is right. If Chile descended into anarchy it makes sense we will too, and when you think that everyone here is armed . . . "

"I'm not armed," Jennifer mumbled.

"Well, maybe you should be. I'd say, head north, get into the Rockies, where there's more space—Canada maybe? I'm sure if you have a head start, you could find an unused cabin. I'd say it would be smart to start driving as soon as you can. Oh, and bring toys and books to educate the little one. Education is important . . . "

"I don't really think everyone is just going to go crazy. I mean, won't people still want to just live their lives?"

"Maybe. But if I'm right—and I might be—it

would be better to find out in the safety of the mountains, no?"

Jennifer thought a little bit, and brushed her brown hair out of her face. "Yeah, I guess you're right. It's going to take us a few days to get ready for this. Then, we'll go."

"Thank you, daughter. Thank you." Robert wiped a tear from his eyes.

11

PLAYING HOOKY

June 14, 2016
Dustin's house, Houston

Jeremy and Dustin looked at the pile of things in front of them. Above the pile was a white board and there was a huge list on the board and almost everything was crossed off of it. On top of the board was the title: "Days until Departure: 2." Jeremy looked over at Dustin, who had his arms half-crossed, rubbing his stubble in thought.

"We have it all?" Dustin asked.

Jeremy looked at the bags. They had a generator, a drill set, a bowie knife, two big tents, rope, plastic bags, matches and lighters and flint, two-way radios, a GPS, road maps, topographical hiking maps, iodine tablets to purify water, waterproof spray, three compasses, an outdoor stereo, ten gallons of water, four water bottles, seventeen packets of Costco Beef Jerky, flashlights, an ax, two big foldable solar panels, clothes for each of them, day backpacks, three utility knives, instant coffee mix, three big boxes of Cliff bars, Gatorade powder, two computers, a book on outdoor hiking, *War & Peace* by Leo Tolstoy, and last but not least, two vintage *Playboy* magazines that Jeremy stole from his dad.

"The only thing I don't understand is the *War & Peace*," Jeremy said, picking up the heavy book. "This thing must weigh like ten pounds."

"Yeah, could come in handy since anarchy might take over. Plus, who knows, it might turn out to be a pretty good weapon."

Jeremy had rented a small U-Haul trailer for one day, and just planned on not returning it, thinking to himself, *The anarchy has begun!*

It was around ten in the morning and he got a text from Anna:

Heyy, I'm at school, can you meet me on the roof?

Unsure of what Anna wanted, Jeremy excused himself from the packing plans, leaving Dustin to put everything in the car.

"Thanks a lot!" Dustin said sarcastically, as Jeremy jumped into his Subaru and sped off toward the high school.

He walked up the stairs to the top floor, passing classrooms until he reached the end of the hall. He and Anna had snuck out onto the roof before; the door was supposedly rigged to an alarm bell but Anna had discovered one day that the system had died long ago. He pushed through the door and walked up the narrow stairs to the roof of the school. All the buildings were situated around the main two-story schoolhouse, so when he reached the roof Jeremy could see the entire high school. He saw the bleachers by the football field, and the scoreboard that yearned to show a victory to its citizens. He saw the baseball diamond, and then all the little heads scurrying around the quad—kids that cut class, kids that had no class.

Anna sat watching the clouds go by.

He walked over to her and sat down. "You okay?" he asked.

Anna leaned on him, and Jeremy put his arm around her. "I just wanted to look out at this view one more time with you," Anna remarked. "Everything seems so calm."

In the distance they could see the Houston skyline, with the blue-orange haze surrounding the tall buildings.

"Yeah," Jeremy replied, "it is."

"I just can't believe—"

Suddenly, a loud *bang!* erupted behind them. Anna yelped in surprise and Jeremy looked behind him. Police sirens wailed.

It's coming from downtown, Jeremy thought.

Jeremy heard gunshots, and the couple looked at each other, both of them having no idea what to do.

Jeremy's phone buzzed.

Dustin: Someone robbed Al's Guns and Ammunition at gunpoint. I think people believe in the comet now. We should go.

Jeremy looked at Anna and showed her the text, and she looked worried, but nodded.

"I haven't even told my parents yet," Jeremy said nervously.

Jeremy texted Dustin back, asking him to pick them up in the parking lot of the school. Jeremy and Anna quickly walked back down the stairs, and waited in the parking lot, crouching behind a car just in case. After ten minutes, they saw the Acura pull up, with the U-Haul trailer behind it. Jeremy couldn't help but chuckle at how the car looked. Its sleek black exterior made it seem like the last car that would be dragging around a scratched and peeling U-Haul trailer.

They quickly scrambled into the car, and drove off toward Karina's apartment, which was just five minutes from school.

"How did you know about the robbery?" Jeremy

asked Dustin as they drove. Now they knew what the super loud sound was—the thieves had used a grenade to bust open the door.

"My aunt texted me. She was across the street when it happened, and saw the whole thing."

Karina was busy packing her clothes—she had skipped school that day, too—and they arrived at her house by one o'clock. She buzzed the group up and they went up in the elevator, which seemed to take forever to get to the fifth floor. Karina answered the door and Anna quickly explained that they needed to go as soon as possible.

"So, are you all packed, or . . . ?" Jeremy asked, eager to get on the road.

"Almost!" Karina replied, showing them to her bedroom.

"Jesus Christ," Jeremy said, while Dustin started laughing.

On the ground beside Karina's bed were two enormous suitcases. Karina could have probably fit in both of them, and one was bulging out the sides.

There was a small mountain of clothes on her bed, which were presumably going into the other half of the suitcase.

Even Anna, whom Jeremy felt had packed twice the amount of clothes that he thought she needed, said, "Kari, you can't be serious."

"I mean, we might not be coming back, and I want to be prepared!"

For six minutes of painful conversation, the four argued about how many clothes Karina was allowed to bring. They settled on letting her bring the bag which was already bursting at the seams, but not until she unpacked and repacked it, this time with some clothes from the other suitcase.

"Better to be prepared!" she said.

Dustin labored to carry the suitcase to the elevator, and down they went. Karina looked nervous and Dustin and Jeremy tried to act brave, but in reality everyone was terrified. Jeremy kept on going back and forth between thinking that either leaving was necessary, or it was the worst idea he'd ever had. Anna grabbed his hand and squeezed it tightly, making him feel secure and happy.

They walked out and got into the car and started to drive north, first stopping by Jeremy's house.

"I have to talk to my parents," he explained. "I have to tell them."

The group waited in the car as Jeremy ran in. *I should have done this sooner,* he thought, chastising himself.

He had a little luck, however, because his mom was feeling a little under the weather and thus had stayed home from work, and his father was home for lunch.

He burst through the door, and saw his father eating a sandwich and his mother drinking a tea.

"Guys," he said breathlessly, "we have to go."

"Where?" his father asked, uninterested.

"Let me start over," he said, taking a deep breath. "A couple months ago, Anna and I found some evidence that NASA had discovered a comet that would collide with Earth and destroy all life and then a week after that, we followed Dr. Miller, a NASA astrophysicist, to a bar where we questioned him and he confirmed what we found and then there was this viral leak of some information about Project Mars—"

"Jeremy, Jeremy, slow down!" his father said, looking over to his wife. It looked like both his parents thought he'd gone crazy.

Jeremy repeated what he said a little slower than he did before, and articulated himself more clearly, but his parents still just stared at him.

"You guys don't believe me?" Jeremy asked angrily. "Dad, I tried telling you this already!"

"Honey," his mother began, "it's not that we don't trust you—we do—but isn't it possible that you're making a few leaps?"

"No—" Jeremy began. "Dad, you saw the JSC. That wasn't normal, right?"

"Of course it wasn't normal," his father began, before looking shyly back at his wife, "but we know why. It's just Project Mars, son."

"Jeremy!" Dustin called from the front door. "Are you ready?"

"Ready for what?" Jeremy's father asked suspiciously.

"I'm leaving to go to a less populated place before the country dissolves into anarchy. Chile is in chaos because they know that a comet is going to hit Earth and destroy everything!"

"Oh no, you are not," Earl said sternly.

"Will you guys please come with me?" Jeremy pleaded one last time, as a last ditch attempt, but his parents just looked at each other, dumbfounded.

"Dustin, start the car, let's go," Jeremy yelled.

"You are not leaving," Earl repeated, unsmiling.

"I love you both," Jeremy said, before stealing a quick hug from his dazed mother. Then he ran after Dustin while his father was too stunned to try and stop him.

• • •

They drove by Al's Guns on their way out of the city. They drove slowly past the police cars parked outside. The tinted glass doors were shattered, and the walls were filled with bullet holes. Jeremy thought that robbing Al's Guns was probably the most dangerous thing to do in all of Houston, even deadlier than robbing a bank. He had gone in there a few times to shoot targets with his father, and imagining someone going in there with guns to rob the place seemed beyond reckless.

Then Al's was gone, and they drove silently forward.

Jeremy didn't know what to say, and apparently the girls didn't either, because everyone remained quiet in the car. Dustin drove in silence. Jeremy turned on the radio and Bob Marley's "Three Little Birds" started playing in the car.

An hour north of Houston they still hadn't seen anything resembling anarchy and decided to stop off for gas. Anna had the idea of taking her father's Visa card, because they figured that in a year or so credit cards would stop working, so they might as well use them while they could. All that mattered now was survival.

They pulled off the freeway and drove into a Chevron, tapped up their supply, and bought two large bags of "Flamin' Hot" Munchie Mix and four Arizona Iced Teas. It turned the mood in the car one-hundred-eighty degrees.

"Awesome, thanks Jer!" Anna said, kissing him on the cheek.

As Jeremy climbed into the passenger seat, he saw a man waving at him, walking toward their car. Jeremy looked behind him to see if the man was waving at someone else. Nope. He looked back at the man, who was tall, maybe six foot four, and his right hand was covered under his jacket.

"Hey, hey!" The man said, in a friendly tone.

"Jer . . . " Anna began, "maybe we should . . . "

"Yeah, man, get in the car." Dustin said nervously.

"Hi fellas, hey!" The man was getting closer.

"Get in the car, Jeremy, get in the car now!" Dustin yelled.

But Jeremy was transfixed by the slow-moving giant and he felt like he was moving in slow motion himself, like the guy had put him under some kind of spell. Jeremy watched the man moving slowly toward the car, and saw the man's expression change from the jovial friendly smile to a determined glare.

Then he saw the reflection of something metal in the man's hand, but still he could not move. Then he felt Dustin's hand on his shoulder. The contact broke the spell. He jumped in the car and yelled, "Go, go, go!"

As he looked back he saw the man aiming a hand-gun at the car. Dustin quickly put the car into gear, and shot out of the gas station. Jeremy heard the loud sharp bang of the gun, followed by Karina screaming and all four of them lowering their heads.

Jesus, the world's going crazy, Jeremy thought.

They made it unscathed to the freeway, and then everyone glared at Jeremy.

"I'm sorry, guys," Jeremy continued, "I don't know what happened. Is everyone okay?"

Karina, Anna, and Dustin all nodded, and Jeremy silently thanked the fact that no one was hurt. He looked outside the car to be sure, once they were far away from the gas station. He stuck his head out of the window to check the side of the car.

There was a bullet hole in the side of the door. Jeremy turned white.

"See anything?" Dustin asked, curious.

"There's a hole in Anna's door."

"Let's be more careful from now on, everyone. No one goes anywhere alone anymore. Buddy system all the time, okay?" Dustin said, keeping his eyes on the road.

"And let's make sure that everyone we meet, no matter how nice they seem, we have to be suspicious of them. We trust only each other. We have each other's backs. We can trust only each other," Jeremy added.

They all agreed, and then they were silent for a

minute. Then, Jeremy could hear Anna softly sobbing in the back. Within ten seconds all four of the group were crying. Sometimes, after a stressful situation, a good cry is what a person needs. Suddenly, Jeremy felt his phone buzz. A private number was calling him.

"Hello?"

"Jeremy? It's Robert Miller, the scientist."

"Oh, hi, Dr. Miller." Why would Dr. Miller be calling him? "Uhhh, what's up?"

"Where are you? Did you take my advice?"

"Yeah, we decided to go north," Jeremy replied.

"Great. Listen, I need some advice. My daughter, Jennifer, is going up north as well. I wanted to give her your information. She is going with her daughter, and if they need anything I'd like you to help them, if you can. Likewise, if you need something, you can trust her. I'm sending you the coordinates of her destination, and her phone number."

"I'll do what I can, doctor," Jeremy replied slowly.

"I have to get back to work. Sorry I'm not much

for the pleasantries now. We have two days until we publish the news. Looks like things are already deteriorating here."

Jeremy thought back to the man who shot at them at the gas station, and a shiver ran down his spine. "Right. Dr. Miller?"

"Yes?"

"Thank you for everything. And good luck saving the planet."

Dr. Miller was silent on the phone for a long time and Jeremy pressed the phone into his ear a little more, so he could hear him, but the line went dead.

12

THE STATE OF THE EARTH ADDRESS

June 17, 2016
Houston, Texas

Earl Genser watched from his television with a beer in his hand as the baseball game switched suddenly to a surprise address by the President of the United States, Victoria Chaplin. He raised his eyebrows, intrigued, and watched:

"Good evening, fellow Americans and citizens of the world. I speak tonight for the destiny of humanity, for the fate of all life on Earth, indeed for the very existence of our beloved planet." President Chaplin looked stoic and calm, and Earl sat up in his chair, furrowing his brow.

"Earlier this week the hacker known as One

Union Anarchist published a document which alleged that our mission to Mars is a cover for a different mission. These allegations are true."

Dr. Miller, who sat in the front row of the press room, shifted uncomfortably in his seat, feeling unnatural in his suit. Some of the reporters tried to ask questions, but President Chaplin continued:

"Please hold all your questions until I have finished. Months ago, astrophysicists at the Johnson Space Center used radio telescopes to confirm the existence of Comet J312, a comet forty kilometers wide, and a comet on a *collision course with Earth*."

President Chaplin said the last words methodically and evenly. Living rooms around the world were quiet, bars fell silent, and newsrooms around the world exploded. The hacker known as One Union Anarchist smiled grimly behind his computer screens. "Comets are volatile, unpredictable, and difficult to spot. There is a small chance that this comet will not come in contact with Earth. But we must plan for an impact. The comet will reach

Earth sometime in June 2018. Interplanetary missiles, initially disguised as the primary supply missions to Mars, will reach the comet shortly and attempt to divert its path. An international team of the world's best scientists are working around the clock to do everything in their power to stop the comet."

Another flurry of questions came from the press. President Chaplin held up her hand and waited for it to die down before saying, "I'd like to introduce Dr. Robert Miller, head of NASA's comet research division. He will be heading the global effort to keep Earth alive."

Dr. Miller felt all eyes on him, even if the cameras hadn't reached him yet.

"We will be providing Dr. Miller's team with everything he needs. Our entire country will be fueling this project. We will turn our military, our financial centers, our auto industry to face this crisis. We will turn Hollywood and Silicon Valley toward this. We will turn Los Angeles and New York toward this. We have the might of the United States of

America and the world, and we must remain a united force against the most Herculean challenge our world has ever faced. It is important to know that the rest of the world will be looking to us as an example, as a beacon of calm, logic, and rationality in this trying time.

"Now, before I turn this over to Dr. Miller," the president continued, "I will take a few questions. Please leave all scientific questions for Dr. Miller."

A fat woman in the front row spoke up. "Thank you, Madam President, Lexy Smith, CNN. You deliberately deceived the American people about the meteor, why?"

The president paused, and then spoke. "We felt that, in the interest of national security, and in order to adequately address the crisis, we needed to be able to focus solely on creating a scientific response team to destroy the comet. If we told the public right away, we would have had to divide our resources. Because we were able to coordinate a planned attack against the comet, we are already defending our planet. The most important task for the world right now is to defend the world against the comet."

There was some unsettled rumbling. It was the sound of a press room full of people who had been lied to.

The president nodded at a smaller man who held a pencil in his raised hand. "John Goodman, Fox. Do the recent uprisings in the Third World, and the lack of communication with the countries of South America, have anything to do with this?"

"The citizens of Chile, upon learning about the meteor, set fire to their capital, Santiago, and within one month, their government had dissolved. We did everything we could to make sure that did not happen here."

Back at the Genser home, Jeremy's father could hear the reporters' gasps. He was watching the television, mouth agape, wondering why he hadn't listened to his son.

Anna's mom held the goodbye note Anna had

written her, while looking at the TV through teary eyes.

Someone else was asking the president a question. " . . . the economy. Are you saying we are going to see a similar shift in the economy like when the United States militarized for the Second World War?"

"The militarization of the economy before World War II was necessary to defeat Nazi Germany, and the United States succeeded in doing that. This is a new enemy—one that no one has ever faced before— and there is no room for error. A comet is coming, and we are the only hope to stop it. Because of this, major car companies like GM, Ford, and Chrysler have all agreed to begin working solely on satellites and other pieces of equipment we will need to ensure the survival of the planet."

As she spoke, around the United States, people were losing their faith. San Francisco and Seattle had already declared national emergencies, and the military swept in, taking control.

"Now, I turn it over to Dr. Robert Miller, the lead

scientist for Project Earth, the global fight against the meteor."

President Chaplin looked over to Robert, who stepped forward. He had never thought in his entire life that the president of the United States would introduce him—much less to the entire world. The room felt very dim and heavy to him, and it was difficult to move. He slowly walked with his papers to the podium and looked at the teleprompter, which was blank.

He looked out over the crowd, aware that all of the lights were on him, but it still felt dim. After what seemed like ten minutes to Robert, he got the courage to speak, and began with something very unimportant.

"Thank you, President Chaplin. First of all, I noticed the press calling this comet a 'meteor.' What is traveling toward us is not a meteor, but a comet. Comets are big, frozen rocks that are typically found in the Kuiper belt, which is about two-point-six billion miles away from us. As the comet gets closer to the Sun, its outer edges will start to melt, giving off a tail of material. These melting regions will play a part in moving the comet's path.

"The comet itself is orbiting the Sun, like everything else in our solar system. It was knocked by another comet some time ago, and this gave it an entirely new orbital path. Within twenty-four months it will come close enough to Earth that we cannot risk doing nothing."

The fat woman from CNN, who had been jumping on her butt in her chair, jumped in quickly to ask a question when Robert took a breath. "Is there a possibility of the meteor landing in the Pacific Ocean, affecting only coastal areas due to a resulting tsunami?"

"Unfortunately, a comet the size of J312 will penetrate the crust of the Earth, and the debris the comet will release into the atmosphere will increase the temperature of the earth by thousands of degrees centigrade within a few days. If this comet hits, all life on Earth will be destroyed, except perhaps some species of protozoa," he said to an increasingly quieter audience. Robert stood uncomfortably behind the podium, knowing what he was about to say would change history. "So it doesn't matter where it will make impact. It will destroy all life on planet Earth if it lands."

"What, exactly, is our plan of attack?" a man from Al-Jazeera asked.

"Comets like J312 have a lot of frozen material inside them. As they get closer to the Sun, some of that material melts, and the gas that's under the outer layer can shoot out, kind of like a jet, which can act to propel the comet. We plan to use this phenomenon to push the comet out of Earth's path.

"We will be using nuclear weapons to force these jets to shoot in strategic locations around the comet, which will slowly move the comet out of its collision course with Earth. We are also using all the technology available to track the comet and model its expected trajectory."

"How likely is a collision event?" someone asked,

while the rest of the room held its breath. To Robert, the air in the room seemed to get even heavier.

"We believe . . . " He trailed off and looked back to the president, who silently urged him to give the world confidence, but Robert was conflicted. *Should I give false hope or tell the truth?*

"The comet is very large," he began, "but we have a lot of weapons on our side. And if the world unites against the comet, we have a good chance of survival."

"Is there a percentage of likelihood of impact?"

Yes, he thought, *ninety-nine percent.* "No," he replied, feeling his gut churn at the lie.

"Your best guess."

Robert sighed. "Next question, please."

It seemed that the media was processing the information themselves, and were also unsure what to say or ask. A few reporters even left the room.

A younger reporter stood up then and addressed Robert. "The One Union Anarchist leak used the name 'Shiva.' This is the name NASA has made for the comet?"

Robert smiled. "Yes, well, no. It's not so much NASA as myself and a few other coworkers . . . "

While Robert responded to the question, Suri imagined the faces of the reporters talking to him. Every one of them probably had that look of dreadful disbelief—the kind of look you only make when you learn that Earth's expiration date is around five billion years early. She had decided to stay home and be with her family while the announcement was made, and she hugged her little sister as they sat on the couch with their parents, watching as President Chaplin returned to make some closing remarks.

• • •

Thousands of miles away, in Torrance, California, Gerald Jan looked over his SpaceX factory, his arms folded, admiring his newest creation. It would be ready for testing soon. Even Mr. Jan was impressed by what the engineers at SpaceX had created to stop Shiva from destroying the world. Dr. Robert Miller and the rest of NASA would need to know about his creation soon.

Jeremy and the crew sat under a tree next to their campsite in the Sam Houston National Forest, drinking water. For a brief second it seemed as though they were just camping, having a break from high school, and enjoying the warm Houston night . . . except that the president had just broken the news about Shiva to the world. They'd watched it on Dustin's phone.

Without talking, the four friends got ready for bed. They had a long drive to make tomorrow, miles to go before they slept. In fact, it would be a long time to go before any of them would sleep soundly again.